DRAFT OF ETERNITY

Victor R. Emanuel

DRAFT OF ETERNITY

VICTOR ROUSSEAU

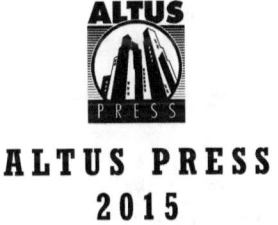

ALTUS PRESS
2015

© 2015 Steeger Properties, LLC, under license to Altus Press • First Edition—2015

EDITED AND DESIGNED BY
Matthew Moring

PUBLISHING HISTORY
"Draft of Eternity" originally appeared in the June 1, 8, 15, and 22, 1918 issues of *All-Story Weekly* magazine (Vol. 84 No. 4–Vol. 85 No. 3). Copyright © 1918 by The Frank A. Munsey Company.
"About the Author" originally appeared in the March 21, 1931 issue of *Argosy* magazine (Vol. 219 No. 5). Copyright © 1931 by The Frank A. Munsey Company. Copyright renewed © 1958 and assigned to Steeger Properties, LLC. All rights reserved.

THANKS TO
Chad Calkins, Joel Frieman, Chris Kalb, and Morgan Wallace

ISBN
978-1-61827-185-3

Visit *altuspress.com* for more books like this.
Printed in the United States of America.

TABLE OF CONTENTS

CHAPTER I

THE PATIENT IN ROOM 9

JAMES MORELAND'S APPEARANCE in the house sur-
geon's room in his private hospital was so rare an occurrence
that I got out of my chair with alacrity, expecting some important communication. I had just settled myself for night duty
and hoped for an uneventful spell. But in a moment I saw that
the famous physician was only in one of his frequent moods of
irritation.

"Look at this, Clifford!" he exclaimed, holding out a small
bottle containing a tincture. "Useless! Perfectly useless! It's a
shame those people in Bombay can't pack their drugs without
their fermenting or spoiling. And that's the sole bottle of
genuine *Cannabis indica* in New York at the present moment,
and all that there's likely to be until the war's ended."

I took the vial from Moreland and held it up to the light.
But this procedure was unnecessary, for the contents were obviously spoiled. It had been badly tamped with cotton wool,
the tincture within the glass was discolored, and even through
the stopper the sweet and rather cloying odor of fermentation
was perceptible.

"It certainly has gone bad, sir," I said. "But I imagine that we
can get all we want at Heiniker & Co."

"Not the genuine *Cannabis*, Clifford," answered Moreland,
sitting down in a chair. "There's plenty of what the pharmaco-
peia calls *Cannabis*. But it can only be prepared properly in the
Orient, and beyond producing a mild species of intoxication

the home-manufactured drug is useless at least for our purposes."

James Moreland's private hospital was devoted to the treatment of nervous maladies of an obscure nature. Moreland was
unique among his contemporaries in that, at the age of sixty,
after having achieved a huge practise as a fashionable doctor,
he had swung about and adopted methods which were decid-
edly old-fashioned.

And yet they were the newest of the new. He began by ac-
cepting certain propositions advanced by the Freudian school,
with its implications of a subconscious life, or what might be
termed a "soul"—doctrines sufficiently unorthodox for his contemporaries to fight shy of him, though his fame prevented
their attaching to him the term charlatan. But, having done
this, with all its corollaries of hypnotic treatment and suggestion, he had gone back to medieval times by declaring that every
ailment had its remedy in some herb of the field.

Our collection of strange tinctures and elixirs would have
dignified the shelves of a master alchemist. Continually I was
in the laboratory, preparing extracts to be tried upon some
patient for some obscure disease. And our results were almost
wonderful enough to justify Moreland's methods.

Such a situation as the one which now confronted us irritated Moreland beyond measure. He sat back in his chair, his
heavy, gray eyebrows drawn together in a frown which did not
relax for nearly half a minute.

"Well, we must trust to Chandra Pal picking up some more
for us when he gets back to India," he said at length. "It will
mean three months' delay, and I expect Mrs. Staines will have
got tired of us by then and gone home, delirium and all, or
found some more orthodox physician. Still, there will be others."

Chandra Pal was a young graduate of Johns Hopkins, who
had been taking a course under Moreland before returning to
his native land. Black as a silk hat, he was thoroughly a gentle-
man, and his knowledge was extraordinary, not only of medicine,

but of the literature of his Sanskrit forebears. He had declined several lucrative offers to remain in America.

"It's most annoying about that *Cannabis indica*," continued Moreland. "Just as alcohol, and nothing else, produces the peculiar symptoms known as drunkenness, so this extract of hemp is the sole means of evoking a specific train of psychic symptoms which, in my opinion, give us the key to many morbid states of the brain. Hashish, you know, gave its name to the sect of Hashashin, which, in turn, has come into our language in the word assassin.

"These Hashashin, who flourished in Syria about the time of the early crusades, were capable of extraordinary deeds under the influence of the hemp drug. They endured terrible tortures with the utmost fortitude and complacency. But it was from reading accounts of their specific illusions that I formed the idea of obtaining a supply of the genuine drug and trying it out here. What should you say is its most remarkable property, Clifford?"

"I understand that, like opium, it abolishes the sense of time," I answered.

"Exactly; but one can hardly say that of opium, which merely stupefies, and so renders its victim unconscious of the lapse of time. The hasheesh devotee lives through centuries in the course of a single moment.

"Of course, as Chandra was saying to me only yesterday, we must admit the truth of the philosophical dictum that time is nonexistent, from the fact that the mind is wholly unable to grasp either infinitely or finiteness, but recoils from each idea in terror.

"However, setting philosophy aside, here is a door leading immediately into that unknown garden, the human soul. Here, by means of a few drops and a hypodermic syringe, we might grope our way into its dim recesses. And to think that those fools of manufacturers have balked us!" he ended vehemently.

He rose and straightened his broad back, and every trace of irritation vanished from his face, which was singularly benign.

"We'll do it yet," he said. "By the way, Clifford, I've been waiting for your week-end vacation to ask you to Northtree. My daughter recently came home from school in Paris, and I'm trying to grow young again for her, and have young people about me. Can you come out Saturday evening?"

This was a mark of strong favor. The few of the staff who had visited the chief came back with stories of hospitality and boredom. But the daughter was a new element.

And she did not interest me in the least. I had had few companions in my early life, had been educated at a semi-charitable school, and had fought every inch of my way toward success. Now twenty-eight found me on its threshold, and utterly weary of everything.

Johnson, the senior surgeon, had been bothering me to join him in establishing a hospital of our own. He had the money to put up, and I was to be a partner. It was the one chance I should have jumped at, and I had been putting him off for weeks.

Perhaps I had been working too hard, but life had never seemed so somber to me as that afternoon. And I am ashamed to admit that I invented a mythical relative in the country to visit whom I was bound in solemn fulfillment of a promise. I stammered out some story of a maiden aunt, who had been a mother to me, and was rightly humiliated at the way in which Moreland took my refusal. It did not occur to him that my apologies were forced and unreal.

"I'm sorry, Clifford," he answered. "Some other time, then. And, before I go, I want to have another look at Mrs. Staines."

This meant that I was to accompany him. Moreland was something of a regal person: he never went through his hospital unless accompanied by a regular retinue. We ascended the stairs, he detested elevators and gradually drew in a courtier group of internes and nurses, until there were seven of us by the time we reached Room 9.

Moreland rapped at the door, and, as no answer came, opened

it. The nurse in attendance, who had left the room for a moment, saw us, and came hurrying along the passage toward us.

"She's fallen asleep, Dr. Moreland," she said.

Moreland made no reply, but went in, and we followed him.

The patient, Mrs. Roy Staines the wife of a well-known architect of the city, was lying in the bed, apparently unconscious, though her eyes were wide open. She was a handsome woman of about thirty-five, with masses of yellow hair coiling about a somewhat too fleshy throat.

She suffered from an obscure nervous malady, which produced a slight delirium at times, principally at night; but she was well enough by day, and only needed attendance after dark.

As we stood watching her I saw consciousness come back into her eyes. She scanned us severally, and then her glance fell upon me. A most sinister expression came upon her face.

"I have found you, then!" she muttered, and began clenching and unclenching her fingers.

I moved behind Moreland, thinking that the irrational fancy which had singled me out would disappear when I was out of the direct range of her vision. But, to my dismay, she sat up in bed and uttered such a scream as I had never heard.

"Aye, slink away, perjurer!" she cried, stretching out her arms in imprecation. "But, though you fly from me through the seven hells of Buddha, I will find you and bring you to judgment!"

There was something so uncanny in her deliberation that, accustomed as I was to such scenes, I felt a thrill of something like fear. I made my way hurriedly out of the room.

The malevolence of the woman's look, the gleam in her eyes, as if of actual recognition, and of remembrance of injuries done by me, made the bleak corridor seem far friendlier than the well-furnished private room. I was half-way down the corridor when Dr. Moreland came quickly after me. With him was Chandra Pal, though I had not noticed him in the room when I was there.

"Our patient seems to have taken an unaccountable dislike

to you, Clifford," said the doctor, laughing. "Never mind! She'll have forgotten it by morning."

"Oh, yes. Excuse me, doctor, but is there such a thing as forgetting?" inquired Chandra in his habitual tone of gentle irony.

"Well—no," Moreland confessed. "But for practical purposes there is. And we're not concerned with Mrs. Staines's subconscious motives for her outburst except professionally. I have no doubt that the forgotten knowledge of some wrong suffered by her accounts for all these symptoms and, once we have elucidated it, her cure is certain. Don't forget, Clifford, that I shall expect you at Northtree at an early date."

And he hurried away, leaving Chandra Pal and me together, while the rest of the retinue dispersed to their duties.

CHAPTER II

CHANDRA PAL

"**WELL, OLD MAN,** I'm sorry we're going to part to-morrow," said Chandra, who had accompanied me back to the house surgeon's room.

"To-morrow, Chandra?" I exclaimed. "Why, I thought you were to remain with us another couple of weeks!" I exclaimed.

"So I had hoped, but I got letters from India to-day announcing my father's serious illness. He is an old man, and not likely to recover, so I thought I ought to take the next boat for England."

"I'm sorry," I said, and meant it, for I had a sincere liking for the kindly little man, though I was often conscious of depths in Chandra that were not fathomable. "Good luck and no submarines! This won't be good-by, though?"

"Oh, no, I'll see you again before I leave, Basil," said the Indian evasively. He contrived to leave upon my mind the impression that we should not meet again, but that he desired to avoid the ordeal of a final parting.

"I hope if ever you come to Bombay you'll be our guest," he continued. "We can meet over there on an equal footing, while here—"

"Oh, nonsense, Chandra! Put that idea out of your sensitive head!" I answered warmly. "Every home here is open to a man of your attainments, as you well know."

"I heard Dr. Moreland extending you an invitation which he never thought of extending to me," answered Chandra,

7

without, however, a trace of bitterness in his voice. "And once, when I had to go to Northtree on an urgent matter, it did not occur to him to present me to Miss Lucy."

"Well, you know how absent-minded the doctor is," I said.

"Oh, ye-es. Quite so," said Chandra. "And, of course, in my country we are not presented to women—schoolgirls like that."

It was his tone more than the words that seemed to me to inflict a slight slur upon Miss Lucy Moreland. But I had never seen her, and she was nothing to me.

"I do not resent it," continued Chandra. "But it is—it is comical, for the good doctor is totally ignorant of the fact that I am almost as white as he ye-es, comparatively speaking, Basil."

I looked in astonishment at the little man. Chandra's soul was undoubtedly white at least, I thought so then—but his fine Caucasian features looked as if they had been hewn out of ebony.

"Yes—what have you here, Basil?" he continued, taking up the bottle which Moreland had left behind. He smelted the stopper cautiously, then held the bottle up to the electric light. "*Cannabis?* That's the stuff the doctor was so angry about? I heard him telling one of the nurses that he had been disappointed in some drugs."

"Yes. You see, it has spoiled, Chandra. It arrived by mail from Bombay this morning."

"Ye-es," said Chandra. "What do you call this, Basil?"

"Why, *Cannabis indica,* of course."

"Ye-es. But you are wrong, Basil. This *Cannabis* isn't spoiled. A mistake of the packer, that's all, because this stuff is never sent out of India, nor to any but native doctors. It isn't *Cannabis indica* Basil.

"No, my friend. This is *Cannabis sativa,* extract of the male flowers of an allied species of the hemp plant. It is an Indian secret. The Europeans have analyzed and experimented with it, but they have never discovered its properties, because only the male flowers may be used for the drug. They pick all the flowers—and then it is no better than water. The packer made a terrible mistake. It is the genuine hashish, Basil—the kind the Hashashin used."

"You're sure? You aren't joking, Chandra?"

"Not by a long sight. It is used extensively among the hill tribes, and none but them know just how to prepare it."

"Did you ever see it used, Chandra?" I asked, intensely interested.

"Ye-es. Oh, ye-es. Not advisable, Basil, old man. It looks as if chance, as you would call *karma,* has placed a very powerful weapon in somebody's hands. I'll take it away with me and send the doctor what he wants—*Cannabis indica,* which will do just as well for his purposes."

"I don't know about that, Chandra," I answered. "What is the property of this drug?"

"Oh, it—unlocks doors that were meant to be closed. The Ghats have a proverb that when the Great Spirit sealed up the soul of man in prison the key was left on the inside, but hidden in the dark."

"Chandra, what did you mean by telling me that you were as white as Moreland?" I demanded suddenly. "Any connection between that statement and what you are telling me now?"

"Ye-es. Oh, yes, there's a connection. But best not to explain, old man."

"Tell me, Chandra. I've got a couple of hours before I make my rounds. Does this stuff abolish the sense of time?"

Chandra sat down deliberately and leaned toward me, resting his arms upon the arms of his chair. "Time?" he asked, smiling. "Time? All rubbish, my dear Basil. The Indian physician has got beyond ail that nonsense. One has to, unless he wants to be reborn forever, treading the same old mill of pleasure and disappointment, and joy and pain, and final failure. Oh, yes, ye-es, our eyes are opened."

"See here, Chandra, you've hinted at this once or twice before!" I said. "Better explain it all to me before you go away.

Moreland made some such suggestion to me just now, but he was speaking out of Western philosophy, which I suppose you sneer at."

"Oh, no! No sneering," answered Chandra. "Plato and Pythagoras knew all that we know. Only they learned it from us. It came to you through Egypt—the mystic knowledge, you understand, Basil. There's nothing to it, really. Time and space don't exist, you know.

"We conceive space as having three dimensions, because we have the three semi-lunar canals in the inner ear, up against the brain, which give us our sense of balance. But we see time in one dimension—for past, present, and future form the same straight line. Time has really three dimensions, so far as it can be said to exist at all."

"That's a fine theory, Chandra. But how can you support it?" I demanded.

"We-ell, we live in dimension one, breadth. But time has length, too. Didn't you ever live twenty years in a dream of a second? Or did you never wonder whether you could finish a certain job within a given time, and you took out your watch and said, 'it depends on how time goes whether I get through or not'? And if the minute hand moved slowly, you got through, and if it moved fast you gave up and waited for another time."

"Yes, but that's a purely subjective experience, Chandra."

"No, my friend. That was more real than the job itself, on which you were working. By concentrating your mind you opened it to realities. That's what the hashish taker does. Time has no meaning for him, because he makes himself stationary in it."

"Stationary in time, Chandra?"

"Ye-es. Time flies, you know. We don't fly, we stand still. Time flies past and gives us events in sequence. But when we get into dimension two, length, then it just vibrates up and down for us."

"I begin to grasp your meaning, Chandra!" I exclaimed. "How about dimension three—height?"

"Ah," said the little Indian, appearing to hesitate, "that's what I was referring to when I said I was as while as Moreland. But never mind, Basil. Give me that bottle!"

I look the bottle from the table and put it in my pocket. "For Heaven's sake go on!" I implored. "I think I know what you're going to tell me."

"Well, I'll tell you, then," said Chandra. "Dimension three, of time, is dropping through time. Moving backward or forward a few centuries. That's what *Cannabis indica* doesn't do, but *Cannabis sativa* does."

"Chandra," I answered, "the difficulty about that is that if I dropped a few centuries ahead or behind I'd find myself non-existent, or else in a reincarnated body which had not the faintest memory of what it had been in the past, or was going to be the next throw."

"But that reincarnation theory is all bosh, Basil," protested Chandra earnestly, "just a truth put incorrectly for the uneducated, you understand. Not a fraud exactly—no-o—just a substitute for ignorant minds. Listen to me, Basil!" The little man gripped my arm in tense excitement, which ought to have struck me as unnatural.

"You and I have always existed, and always will exist, in bodies, just as we do now. And we are living in hundreds of different bodies at the same time.

"It's a leetle hard, Basil, old man, but in order to understand it you must get the time delusion right out of your mind. When you realize the three dimensions of time you're on the road to enlightenment. But even that's only a working hypothesis. The truth is, there isn't any time. Julius Caesar is being stabbed at this minute in Rome. George Washington is at Valley Forge. I'm a dirty little boy playing in the streets of Bombay, and you're a grandfather dangling his first grandson. Don't you see, Basil? All simultaneous. Everything—ye-es. We see it in sequence because of finite mind.

"You're slave in ancient Athens, and horse-thief in Montana, and doctor here, and king in China, all at same instant. You're cave-man and Eskimo and modern American in different bodies. All depends on where you focus consciousness. *Cannabis sativa* shifts focus of consciousness at will. Give me that bottle!"

I PUSHED him back into his chair. "And so you're perfectly white, Chandra, at this moment, and living in the time of the Pilgrim fathers?" I asked incredulously.

"Ye-es," said Chandra, with a flicker of something sardonic in his answering grin. "Two, three, four hundred years, only ahead, not back. Usually we don't change color or features much in a few hundred years. But I change, because I know the secret. "So you give me that bottle, friend Basil, and I'll take it away, and you forget what I've told you. Here we two are very good friends—oh, yes, ye-es, the very best. In other lives, perhaps no. And it's awfully hard to focus consciousness upon another life, Basil, and then jump back again when we grow tired. And maybe they don't know about *Cannabis sativa* there. And, anyhow, I carry over all my memories, but you carry hardly anything. You're like a man in a dream. Ye-es. That bottle, please!"

I don't know how it was, but I felt carried away by Chandra's extraordinary statements. Looking back now, I can see that I was as if hypnotized by the little man. Dim instincts of boyhood, suppressed for years by the realities of life, rose up in me and clamored for freedom.

"Chandra," I cried, "I'm sick of my life here. What am I? A drudge of a doctor, with long years of drudgery behind me, and longer years to come. I'd give anything, everything, if I could shake this world off my shoulders and go into another time and period."

"You are sure, Basil?" inquired Chandra, looking at me curiously.

"Dead sure. I'd simply disappear, and, after a few days of wonder, they would begin to forget me. My place here can readily be filled—"

"But wait a moment, Basil," protested Chandra. "You haven't understood. You won't disappear. Basil Clifford will go on working here, and marry, and rise to fame, and all—that perhaps marry Lucy Moreland—"

A spasm crossed his face for an instant.

"Ye-es, and all that. But you won't know. You'll have focused consciousness in another of your bodies, that's all. And, as I said, there may be no *Cannabis sativa* there, or you may not remember that you were ever anywhere else."

"Have you ever done this, Chandra?" I asked, and somehow, as I looked into the little Indian's face I could not help believing him.

"Ye-es," said Chandra, hesitating. "In a way, ye-es. All Brahmins can learn. But it's not good to play with."

"Play!" I cried impetuously. "See here, Chandra, this isn't play to me. Here I am, a healthy young fellow, well under thirty, with absolutely no future to look forward to unless I put in another dozen years of drudgery. And I can't do it, Chandra. I've got no ties to inspire me to do it. I've worked like a dog ever since I was a kid. I waited at table to go through college. I've known pretty nearly every hardship and every humiliation. And—I'm sick of it all."

"Ye-es. But what do you want to be, friend Basil?" asked Chandra.

"I want to live in another age, when men could win success by adventure. I want to fight the world, but I don't want to fight as a humiliated, tired-out underdog. I'd like to live in the age of the Vikings, or—"

"Wait a minute," said Chandra, speaking in tones that were quite peremptory when compared with the mildness of his habitual utterance. "I can help you, and I can go with you to show you the way. Yes, yes, yes!" He nodded his head, and again I saw the sardonic look flicker across his face. "But it isn't easy, Basil. Only a few can fix their period exactly. One must focus the mind through the will, by intense concentration you understand. One must picture exactly what he wants to be, and when he wants to live. I can help you, as I said, and still go to India and see my father. But maybe our wills pull opposite ways. Eh, Basil?"

"Help me the best you can," I implored. "Let's fix our epoch as that of Scandinavia about the tenth century. I suppose I lived then?"

"Surely, friend, for the will to return to it is nothing but the submerged memories. Only, don't say 'lived.' Say 'live,' for the Scandinavia of the Vikings is now, not in the past. No past, no future only the present. You understand theory?"

"I do," I answered, taking off my coat.

"Once more you are sure you mean it, Basil? It's a long, long journey."

"I mean it as much as I ever meant anything, Chandra."

"Yet once more. Maybe there's no returning. Probably no. You'll work at hospital, but never know it. Ye-es. And while you fight with Mrs. Staines"—here yet again I saw that smile about his mouth—"really you're pirate on East Anglian coast, burning Saxon farms and herding cattle. Yes? Fine sort of life? All right. It's hard at first, and sometimes failure, but we'll try."

"You won't desert me, Chandra?" I asked, in sudden fear that I would not confess, as I took a hypodermic from its case.

"No, no, friend. I'll stand by you," he replied. "And when you want to remember, maybe I'll help you to remember."

I uncorked the vial and filled the needle till Chandra nodded. Then I corked it, and with an impulse for which I cannot account, I sealed it and slipped it into my pocket. I rolled up my sleeve, and Chandra inserted the needle into the flesh of my upper arm.

Having injected about half the contents, he rolled up his own sleeve and gave himself the remainder.

CHAPTER III

"CANNABIS SATIVA"

BEYOND THE STING of the hypodermic I was conscious of no change. I remember that I was surprised how natural everything seemed.

Chandra was sitting opposite me, wearing his usual placid smile. It irritated me a little that he should take so momentous an event so as a matter of course.

"How long will it be?" I asked him.

But before he had time to answer me I heard footsteps descending the stairs—several pairs of them, as if some one were in flight and others in pursuit. The door burst open, and Mrs. Staines rushed in like a fury.

She flew straight at my throat, but before she could strike me the two nurses who were following hard behind had caught her and held her arms, while she panted and choked with fury.

"Hold him!" she shrieked. "He thinks to escape free after the insult that he has placed upon me, but he does not reckon with the vengeance that shall fall upon him!"

As suddenly as the outburst had begun, it ended. Mrs. Staines subsided and stared stupidly about her, as if not knowing where she was. Her eyes fell upon my face again, but there was no recognition in them. The nurses led her away, and she offered no opposition.

The interruption had been so sudden that, when Chandra and I were together in the room again, alone, I could hardly believe it had occurred.

And nothing had changed—unless—well, I felt as if a film had passed across my brain, and had been withdrawn. I mean that the incursion of Mrs. Staines, real though it had been—as real as anything that ever happened—left the impression of a moving picture. I recall that both the woman and the attendant nurses had seemed flat upon the wall, without perspective. I do not know any better way of describing this impression.

And there was one more thing, which hardly struck me at the time. But against this flat background I had seemed to see the very misty outlines of some huge building—a sky-scraper of some sort—with heaps of rubble about it, as if it were disintegrating under the tooth of time.

Yet these ideas were so hazy that they left no definite impression. I was still sitting in the house surgeon's room, facing Chandra, and Chandra was smiling.

"Well, that's a poor beginning," I suggested.

"What?" inquired Chandra.

"Why, Mrs. Staines bursting in like that!" I cried. "You look as if you hadn't seen her, Chandra."

"Our patient from above came down, did she?"

I was beginning to be alarmed. I fancied now that the whole incident might have been a species of delirium, and yet it had seemed incredibly real.

"You did see her, Chandra, didn't you?" I cried in agitation.

"Oh, Mrs. Staines? Yes, to be sure, Basil, old man. But I didn't quite understand you. Mrs. Staines came into this room—yes, oh, yes. I was trying to test your powers of perception, Basil, that's all."

Instinct told me that he was lying. Yet there was no reason why he should lie. Could it be that the drug had already affected him, while leaving me unscathed? I was growing more and more uneasy. And I was already regretting my folly.

"How long does it take to get into full operation?" I asked.

Chandra shrugged his shoulders.

"My dear Basil," he answered, "that is more than I can possibly tell. It depends entirely upon the focusing of the will, you understand. With some, an hour. With some, instantaneous. With a few, never. But with you—yes, perhaps three or four hours. Possibly a second dose would be required. I can't tell. I warned you, dear friend, that the pathway into the unknown is a perilous one."

He spoke like a man who, deprived of volition, had resigned himself to the workings of fate. Something in his demeanor made me more afraid now than I had ever been in my life.

"If it's a matter of focusing the will," I answered, "I think it might be better for me to make my rounds quickly at once, and then I'll have till midnight."

He only shrugged his shoulders again, and I got up and went out of the room. The familiar entrance hall of the hospital was indescribably reassuring to me.

What a fool I had been to place any credence in Chandra's crazy experiment! At worst, I might expect two or three days of severe sickness and nervous depression as the result of the injection; at best, only a little discomfort. Perhaps an antidote would be advisable.

Nevertheless my purpose in going upstairs can probably be divined. I wanted to make sure that Mrs. Staines had really been into my room.

My heart was beating as I approached the door of her room, and I must have trod heavily, for the nurse—one of the two who had pursued her heard me and came out, finger on lip.

"She's having a good, sound sleep," she said. "She seems better to-night than usual."

"When—when did she fall asleep?" I asked.

"About an hour ago, Dr. Clifford."

"Yes, but—she wasn't walking in her sleep, then?"

You see, I put the question indefinitely enough to arouse no suspicion, whether Mrs. Staines's appearance before me had been a fact or a delirium. But the nurse only looked back at me blankly.

"No, she has never done that," she answered. And then, clinching the matter:

"She fell asleep soon after you were in here last, doctor, and she's rested quite comfortably since, hardly moving."

It was delirium, then! The confounded drug had made a fool of me. And it had not acted in the least as Chandra had suggested. For it had simply called up an imaginary picture which the half-stupefied brain had translated into action through the misleading of the senses.

I went down-stairs with the idea of taking an antidote for the *Cannabis*. I was not sure what would be best. An emetic was useless against a hypodermic; perhaps arsenic, I thought. And I must get Chandra to take some.

Yet, when I reached the house surgeon's room again, something strange about Chandra drove the thought of the antidote out of my mind.

He was standing facing me in the doorway, his hand held out in greeting.

"Well, old man, I'm sorry we're going to part to-morrow," he said.

"To-morrow, Chandra?" I exclaimed. "Why, I thought you were to remain with us another couple of weeks."

"So I had hoped," he replied, "but I got letters from India to-day announcing my father's serious illness. He is an old man, and not likely to recover, so I thought I ought to take the next boat for England."

I staggered back and screamed out in my terror.

"Chandra!" I shouted, "you've told me all this before. Don't you remember? The same words—the same gestures. For God's sake, is it that damned drug, or what's the matter with you?"

I say I shouted this, and yet there stood Chandra before me, repeating the words mechanically, as if he had not heard me:

"I hope if ever you come to Bombay you'll be our guest," he said. "We can meet over there on an equal footing, while here—"

I sat down in my chair, listening to the dreary monologue. I was convinced now that the drug had had a more potent effect upon me than I had imagined. It was not so much Chandra's repetition of his own words that horrified me as that he was repeating his own acts and gestures.

For by some freak of memory I recollected exactly how he had looked, where he had stood before; I knew that a certain expression would come upon his face at a certain sentence; I knew that there would come a pause during which I was supposed to be answering.

I listened to the whole exposition of Chandra's fantastic theory once more. I listened until he stretched out his hand to take the needle which I was presumably extending to him.

Yet I did not know whether he was a fantom of my brain, or whether Chandra had been driven insane by the *Cannabis*. But I was aware of a languor which would not have been displeasing under other circumstances, which prevented me from laying hands forcibly on my tormentor, who listened to no pleas, and seemed not to see or hear me as he addressed the invisible apparition supposed to be myself.

And behind Chandra, growing ever more real, yet still misty and wavering as a moving picture, I saw the ruined tower upon the wall.

Chandra had reached out his hand for the syringe when suddenly I heard footsteps on the stairs, and once more Mrs. Staines burst into the room, the nurses in hot pursuit.

Again she screamed that lunatic invective, and once more the film passed from my brain. This was no dream, but real to the last detail.

It was an exact repetition of what had gone before. Again Mrs. Staines stared at me stupidly till she was led away. And once more Chandra was seated opposite me smiling.

He nodded his head. "Yes, I saw her that time, Basil," he said. "It is as I suspected."

"What?" I cried.

He rose and came toward me and patted my arm, seating

himself upon the arm of the chair in which I was huddled. "Have no fear, Basil, old man," he said.

"Chandra, explain it all to me," I pleaded. "Don't you see—it's not the delirium that I'm afraid of. If I've got to pay for my folly by dying a madman, I'm ready to. But I don't know the reality from the dream."

"No, Basil," said Chandra gently. "It's all right. Don't be afraid. You are well on the path now. This Mrs. Staines was the reality; the first was the dream."

"And you—you—why did you repeat your words?"

"My words, Basil? Did I do that? Excellent. The first was the reality, the second the dream. That is to say, as a working hypothesis. Actually, both are true. You understand, Basil, old man?"

"I understand nothing, except that I have been delirious."

"Why, it's quite clear, if you had followed me. Don't you see? The mind is like an old man in an old house. He doesn't want to have to find other quarters. So the landlord serves notice on him and he doesn't wish to go. When he has to go he looks back regretfully, he lingers near the old house. Pendulum goes to and fro, Basil. When I repeated myself, time pendulum had swung back an hour. When false Mrs. Staines came in the first time, time pendulum had swung forward an hour. You saw an hour ahead, as time goes. That's all."

"You mean that I was living an hour ahead the first time Mrs. Staines entered this room?"

"Surely, Basil."

I rose out of my chair; and now the room seemed ethereal as vapor, and out of it I seemed to see Chandra, taller, fairer, and wearing garments of some iridescent stuff that shimmered like shot silk.

"Better give me that vial, Basil," he said in thin tones that sounded like a distant fife. Or was some one playing the fife, far down the corridor?

"Perhaps we find an antidote," he continued.

"No," I answered. "I'll hold on to that."

I saw a look of dismay cross his features.

"You give me that vial," he insisted.

"No," I answered resolutely. "And see here, Chandra. You've done mischief enough to-night with your accursed experiment. I'm going home to be ill, and I shall ring up Bowyer to take my place here to-night. But I'm going to keep that vial, and to-morrow I shall have the stuff analyzed and find out what's in it. I—"

I broke off in dismay, for the room had faded from my vision, going out like an over-exposed photographic plate in the developing mixture, though I could still feel the carpet under my feet. I turned to face Chandra. He alone was visible, and he stood out against the background of blackness as if illuminated by some phosphorescent fire. I saw the transformation still more clearly. He was wearing what looked like a Mongolian's headpiece. The slightly oblique eyes peered into mine with a look of angry cunning, and the hand that grasped my arm like a vise, yet was hardly felt by me, was lean and clawlike.

"You give me that vial, you fool!" he bellowed in my ear.

Lost as I was, I knew that all my hope depended on my keeping the vial.

And, the moment that final decision came into my mind he read it in my face. He struck at me, but his blow fell light as thistledown. He grasped my throat, and his clutch was only that of a tenuous fantom. He knew that he could not hurt me.

His lemon-colored face was upturned to mine, for, in spite of his heightened statue he was still three inches shorter.

"Basil," he hissed, "I've been a friend to you. You asked my help. I've given it to you. You asked me not to desert you, I won't. I'll keep that promise."

He chuckled viciously.

"Now—I can't get you to take it away. But in the place where you're going I can take it and make you feel what you can't feel now, in intermediate world. Soon I'll get you. Don't think you can escape the vengeance of the Yuki. Timour's long arm was never withdrawn till it had grasped its prey. So you give up that vial and make Timour your friend."

"Yuki!" "Timour!" The names fell upon my consciousness as long familiar ones, growing clearer and ever clearer in my memory. I felt my body shudder, as if they were names of horror, though as yet I could not grasp their significance.

Chandra's body wavered before me like a mist-wraith. Behind him loomed the massive pile of ruined stones. And, flat upon this, like a printed picture, I seemed to see the house surgeon's room in Dr. Moreland's hospital.

Blindly I felt my way toward the door. In some manner I found it. I staggered into the hall and collided with the door of the automatic elevator. Installed but seldom used, since Moreland abhorred it, and it was generally out of order. I pressed the button and got the door open, with a dim idea of escaping from Chandra. I heard the rattle of the ropes above—and suddenly I found myself in utter darkness.

CHAPTER IV

RUUF, SON OF OG

JUST FOR AN instant consciousness seemed to leave me. But I did not fall, and as the sensation of touch came back to me it brought a feeling of keen alertness.

Moreland, New York, Chandra, the hospital were still within the scope of memory, and yet not focused by the brain. They seemed as forgotten dreams in the presence of some threatening peril.

I was standing upright on broken stones. My hands clung to what seemed the masonry of a tunnel, and were wet with moisture from the walls. My sandaled feet ached from the bruising of stones, and I knew that I had come miles along that subterranean passage.

Presently, impelled by the same sense of fear, I continued groping my way forward into the darkness. Now the memory of the past had vanished wholly, and I only knew that a change had come over me. I was not even aware of my own name.

Suddenly there broke out, somewhere overhead, the distant sound of fifes. And, mingled with this came the hoarse, distant roar of a mob, dulled by the tunnel walls.

The archway fell back on either side of me. I stopped, and very gradually a picture began to form in the darkness. It came out to use the same simile that I have already employed like a photographic plate in the developing solution. I saw the outlines of two heads bent over a bowl on a table.

The first head to become distinct was that of an aged man.

He had a long, white beard, and a golden chain connected his wrists, which were handcuffed with golden fetters; but the fetters were light and the chain long enough to allow the free use of the hands, so that these seemed the ornaments of servitude rather than a restraint.

He was clad in a long robe of coarse sacking, a drab garment crudely dyed, girt up about the knees and fastened around the waist with a cord. Upon his feet were woolen sandals.

Then, slowly and mistily, the second head came into view, and I caught my breath in emotion as I looked upon it.

It was that of a girl of about twenty years, the most beautiful, and with the saddest face that I had ever seen. There was intense pathos upon it, but there was also the restraint of a strong nature, even imperiousness, I thought. She wore what seemed to me layer upon layer of white silk, sheer as cobwebs, massed and heaped about her like sea-foam.

These many garments were buckled at the waist with a clasp of gold. Her arms, bare to the elbows, were white as snow, and great gold bracelets were clasped about her wrists. Her fair hair was fastened about her head in shining coils beneath a coronet.

The moment that I set my eyes upon her face I felt a vast relief, as if I had met a friend at the end of my strange and mysterious journey. I knew that the purpose of my journey had been to meet her, though the place from which I had set out was forgotten. I knew that, in seeing her. I was only renewing a knowledge of her that transcended time.

She seemed one whose life had been indissolubly linked with mine through eons past.

Behind the two I saw the outlines of the cavern come into view. It was a sort of den under the rocks, roughly divided into sections by natural projections from the walls, which had been built out with stones and debris to form several incomplete chambers, as if for a community.

Couches of skins were on the ground. There was a pot, simmering over a fire, and the low table with the bowl of water, into which the two were looking.

From the far end of the cave, which was hidden in darkness, there came the distant sound of hammering, as if on an anvil. From overhead the sound of the fifes still reached me, but the voices of the mob, which had mingled with them, were no longer audible.

The two figures continued to look intently into the bowl of water upon the table.

"Surely, Malachi," said the girl, with a touch of impatience in her voice, "your magic arts have not deserted you? You know the great danger that I have risked in stealing away from the palace, in order to come here, that I may not become the bride of the accursed Timour, of the cruel Yuki."

The names went through my head now as if they were perfectly familiar to me. The speech, which was a clipped English, was comprehensible, and yet it gave me the impression of being a foreign tongue that I had mastered, and not my own.

"That need never be, O Princess Alma," answered the old man.

"It shall not be," she replied, "so long as I have the last resource—the sealed vial that my ancestors have handed down to the princesses of the captivity, lest any of them be constrained to mate with the accursed Yuki rulers."

"Think not of that, O princess," answered Malachi. "If the deliverer whom I have summoned obeys the task laid upon him, all shall be well, and the Yuki driven from the land forever. But if he fails, then the people of the captivity shall be ground down yet more under the Yuki rule."

"Let him not fail, then," murmured the girl, "for rather than wed Timour I would break and drink of the vial, no matter what the issue. Surely he cannot fail, for all our traditions tell us that his day is at hand!"

"Hush!" said the old man, raising his hand in warning. "Look into the bowl!" And, stretching out his arms in invocation, until the gold chain creaked as it grew taut against the fetters, he cried:

"By the unspoken name! By the words of our sires, written in the secret books! By the prophecies that cannot be broken, I summon thee! I call upon thee! Come forth out of the night in which thou dwellest, waiting to fulfill thy task, deliverer of the captive people! Come forth, and show thyself to me in the smoke of the water!"

As he spoke I saw a thin mist begin to curl upward out of the bowl. I watched the scene in increasing amazement; for, though I could see the pair plainly, it was clear that I was wholly invisible to them. The cavern was illuminated by the light cast from rushes set in sockets upon the walls. Yet, standing immediately in front of them, I saw their eyes wander toward me as if I were not there.

Then the smoke from the bowl, drifting toward me as if blown by a fan, enveloped me. It clung about me, hiding everything from my sight. The faces faded.

Suddenly it seemed to be gathered together, as if two hands had seized it. It formed a sort of frame about me. I saw their faces—and they saw mine.

I saw the girl's eyes, fixed on mine in wonder and fear, dilate. Then she leaned toward me with outstretched arms.

"Touch him not!" thundered old Malachi, hobbling between us and waving her back. "Wait—for he is not yet of flesh and blood, even as we!"

But, with the intense yearning of one who finds a long-sought loved one, I reached out my arms toward the girl. I touched her finger-tips; and then she was kneeling before me and pressing my hand to her lips. And the smoke vanished through the cave.

"Rise, O princess! It is well! It is well!" chuckled old Malachi. "Come hither, wanderer, and have no fear! Rise, O princess, for it is not seemly in one of the royal blood to pay obeisance thus!"

The girl rose, and seemed to see my face more plainly as the smoke vanished. I saw a fleeting terror, mingled with something like aversion, upon hers. She started back, and began to whisper anxiously into Malachi's ear.

"It matters nothing," answered the old man. "His mother was of our people." And, turning to me, he asked:

"What do you remember?"

His question raised aching doubts that I could not still. I looked at him in utter bewilderment. Far back among the avenues of memory a faint light seemed to shine, but even as I sought for it, it went out. And two sets of identities, two histories, utterly distinct, seemed to be struggling in my brain. They neutralized each other: my past, before I entered the cave, was a total blank.

My looks must have been eloquent of my thoughts, for old Malachi turned again to the princess and said:

"It is even as I foretold. He remembers nothing. Do you believe now that this is truly he, destined to save our people, O princess?"

"I believe," she answered in a low voice, fixing her frightened eyes on mine.

"Yea, this is he," cried Malachi, "whom I have summoned at the appointed hour, out of timeless space, as our prophets foretold. And he remembers nothing, which was to be the sign. Have patience, O princess, and all shall be made clear. And now you must go, for dawn approaches, and there is much to be done: nor must you fail to be in the women's apartments when Og wakes from his sleep and summons you."

The girl turned to go; but, before she went, she made a low obeisance to me, raising her eyes to mine; and in their depths I read that I frightened her no longer. I read more; something that thrilled my whole being with joy. For I saw there the same recognition which I had felt as if our spirits, long related, had known each other in some eternal life beyond the prison of flesh.

She went slowly out of the cave in the direction of the hammering sound, which was now more distinct. And my eyes, used to the darkness, detected the faint reflection, upon the walls of the cave, of the smiths' fires.

Malachi came up to me, took me by the hands, and peered into my eyes.

"My arts have not failed me," he began. "You, destined to save the captive people from the tyranny of the cruel Yuki—you I have called out of the depths of time to fulfill your task.

"Ages ago—so our tradition runs—these mighty ruins of Nork were built and inhabited by men of the white race. They became luxurious and evil, and fell before the Yuki from the frozen north, who condemned them to toil for them as workers of iron and armor-makers.

"But the royal line of the captive people remains. The Princess Alma has grown to womanhood in the palace of Og, the usurper, with her half-sister Kara. He has betrothed her to Timour, the Yuki prince, who has arrived to carry her away to his own land.

"Because our people are too dispirited to save her, it was necessary to summon one who should lead us. Our secret books have long foretold his coming. You, then, I have summoned here to undertake this task. Are you willing?"

"Yes!" I cried eagerly. For it seemed to me that I had come upon this journey, whose beginning was hidden from me, by my own volition; and that it was for Alma's sake.

"Yet understand that this is no light task which you accept," continued Malachi. "There is a struggle before you, and an inevitable choice, and you will win the prize and yet lose the prize, and win the prize again, though not in the way you hope. If you are courageous, all will be well.

"Now you must learn who you are, in order that you may carry out the task which has been laid upon you. There is a prophecy, of immemorial age, in the royal line of the Yuki, which says that the great Yuki Empire shall fall by the act of one of its own house, whose mother shall be a woman of the white ant-people, as they call us.

"Your father, the great King Og, who dwells in the palace above us, loved a white woman, a captive taken in one of his forays, many years ago. When he learned that she had become the mother of a son, he feared that the ancient prophecy was about to be realized.

"It was in his mind to put you to death, but, yielding to the entreaties of your mother, whom he still loved, he had you sent to a remote part of his kingdom, by the seashore, and brought up by an old peasant, warning him under pain of death never to reveal to you your name or estate.

"Six months ago your old foster-father revealed this to you upon his death-bed. You, who had grown to manhood thinking yourself a swineherd's son, were Ruuf, the son of Og, the mightiest monarch on earth.

"The old swineherd gave you a ring, which your mother, dying, had secretly sent to him. King Og had once promised her that he would grant any petition of its wearer, unto the half of his kingdom. Behold it!"

He pointed to my hand, and, extending it, I saw a gold ring on my finger, set with a flaming ruby.

"A month ago," continued Malachi, "the report came to King Og's ears that his son was still alive, although your foster-father, fearing for your safety, had assured him of your death in childhood. In his old age Og's heart yearned for you. He sent messengers to bring you to Nork, and, believing that they would return with you, ordered a seven days' festival in your honor, and betrothed you to the Princess Kara, half-sister to Alma, hoping by this double marriage of the two princesses to strengthen his throne.

"But Timour, who covets the throne of Og, and feared you, sent messengers to waylay and kill you on your journey. You were warned and escaped them, but, knowing that Timour's men watched all the roads, and Og's messengers having been scattered by Timour's band in the guise of robbers, you entered a tunnel shown you in your sleep, through my arts, hoping to reach your destination thereby. This you have accomplished. And you remember nothing of this?"

"Nothing," I answered.

Old Malachi placed a withered hand upon my shoulder.

"Hard is the test, my son, and yet it must be borne," he said. "Look into the water-bowl!"

I looked, and the vision brought back my memories. I saw myself, a boy in the swineherd's hut, my youth, my foster-father's death, Og's messengers, and all the adventures on the road to Nork.

And, remembering everything, I started up eagerly.

"I am a king's son!" I cried. "I care nothing for you and the white ant-people who toil for us among these ruins. Beware lest Og's vengeance fall upon you for having lured me hither to compass your designs!"

Old Malachi chuckled. "Look into the water-bowl once more, my son!" he said.

I looked, unwilling, yet unable to resist the command. And this time a different set of pictures flashed out before my eyes.

I saw my life in New York from the days when, a poor boy, I waited at table to earn the money to pass through college. I saw the interminable struggle, my graduation, my first patients, the final success, my appointment to Moreland's Hospital; lastly the scene in the house surgeon's room, with Chandra and myself taking the hypodermic. And I remembered all.

I cried out in humiliation and anguish. The dual picture, stamped on my brain, seemed to rob me of personality. It made life seem unreal as a dream. But Malachi pointed to the water-bowl once more, and again, under the same compulsion, I gazed into its unruffled surface.

This time I saw nothing but my own reflection. I saw a young man attired in a plain garment of coarse black cotton, with a girdle about the waist and sandals on my feet. Upon my head was a white cotton turban, and the somberness of my attire was relieved only by a pheasant feather that trailed down over my shoulder from the turban's peak.

As I stared at the reflection in amazement Malachi drew me away and patted my shoulder kindly.

"Think not of yourself, Ruuf, but of your task," he said. "If you accept, an inner guidance will be given that will enable you to surmount all obstacles."

"I accept!" I cried. "But rid me of these past memories, which haunt me."

"They are already half forgotten," he answered, "and will be recalled only when it is to your interest that you should remember."

As he spoke the memories of New York began to fade away, leaving those of the swineherd's but predominant.

"If, now, you accept this charge, O Ruuf, son of Og," said Malachi, "place your hand between the parchments of this book and swear it!"

I placed my hand upon a page of the heavy, leather-bound volume which he put before me, repeating some words which he uttered in the archaic Yuki, which, however, conveyed little impression to me.

"As to your instructions," said Malachi, "you need know nothing, save that, when the time arrives for you to play your part in overthrowing the Yuki, such things as are to be done will be conveyed to your knowledge. But know, O son of Og, that in this life you are young. Many are the lures to faithlessness. Hold steadfast, and resist, that you may accomplish that which has been laid upon you."

CHAPTER V

TIMOUR, PRINCE OF NORK

WITH A GESTURE of his hand he indicated to me that I was to accompany him into the recesses of the cavern.

Soon the darkness began to be illuminated by the red glow of fires. These grew brighter, the heat, of which I was already conscious, intense; the hammering grew louder till it was deafening; and we came upon a vast pit, fitted crudely as a foundry, in which a thousand men were toiling. I had already begun to speculate upon the nature of the Yuki civilization—not as one from another age, but in my dominant guise of a youth from the country, wondering at the sights of the metropolis. I saw that its characteristic was the enormous scale on which everything was built. The rude mechanism was on an imposing scale. The iron pieces were of huge thickness. The great hammers, plied by the silent slaves, and often wielded by half a dozen men, fell in unison upon the white-hot ends of iron bars as thick as girders.

The naked bodies of the workmen, grimed though they were with soot, and scorched and seared by coals, I could see to be those of white men.

At another gesture from Malachi I looked upward. I perceived a structure straddling the pit, and walling it in circular form, which took my breath away; for it seemed to have been built by giants.

The pit itself seemed to have been hollowed out of a deposit of masonry debris, the wreck of the Titanic labors of some prehistoric race of builders. Round it rose the walls of a great hollow tower, or well, of dazzling whiteness, narrowing toward the top in fact, as well as in perspective. Half-way between the summit and the pit, perhaps five hundred feet overhead, the white walls, illuminated by the glow from the furnaces, swelled into a sphere, ringed with a platform, on which a few tiny figures were moving.

This central well was set into the great palace of Og, the wonder of the world, whose innumerable interior windows leered out of the white walls like eyes in a grinning bone. That is the only metaphor I can find to describe the effect of those uncountable windows all the way up the great white interior shaft, tapering from its vast circumference, above the pit's edge, to the top, where it seemed to enclose a rim of roof no larger than a coin. And all up the white well from the pit to the central rotundity danced and played shadows of men, vast silhouettes that leered and writhed and beckoned like the fantasms of a disordered brain.

"All this iron," said Malachi, pointing to a pile of metal, "was dug elsewhere and fashioned into these broken walls to uphold them, by the builders of another age, who did not dream of the use to which it would be put by their slavish descendants. Come with me!"

He led me up a stone stairway that ran up one side of the pit. At the top was a door of iron, built on the same huge scale, set into a wall of masonry which surrounded the hollow. Before it stood two Yuki bowmen, each with a bow as high as himself, and a sheaf of arrows on his back.

Malachi uttered some countersign, and we passed them. The old man took from his girdle a key of iron, two feet in length, and fitted it into a great lock. He turned it by the exercise of considerable muscular power, and pushed open the door, which swung slowly upon its hinges.

"Ruuf, son of Og," said Malachi, "heir of two ages, thus the door opens for you out of the past into the future, seen dimly

by me, but unknown to you. Go forth into your father's
kingdom!"

And he was gone, while the ponderous door clashed fast
behind me, leaving me standing on the outer side of the pit.

I looked about me. The scene seemed to strike some chord
of my forgotten memories, and for a few minutes these blended
with those of my present life, blurring the picture and confus-
ing me.

In the pale light of the dawn I saw a vast city of stone, built
high upon a foundation of ruins, so that the streets which ran
between the rows of houses were like canons.

These ruins extended as far as the eye could reach. Standing
at a considerable height, on the outer rim of the pit, I was able
to take a comprehensive view of my surroundings.

The dead city of Nork was built between two broad rivers,
not a great distance apart, which ran into an almost circular bay
of great extent. The men who had built it in some prehistoric
age had spanned the lesser river with five or six bridges, whose
massive towers stood up, almost intact, on each side of the shore,
although the intervening spans had been swept away.

But across the interval between the two massive stone towers
of the bridge nearest me a slender pathway had been suspended from shore to shore, evidently much later than the original
structure, and too light by far for the towers that held it. Across
this an endless procession of camels was passing from the outlying regions into Nork. Beyond the river I saw ruins again,
crowning a ridge.

The mighty palace of Og was in itself almost a little city. It
towered above me, with its foundations set far into the ruins
beneath, its innumerable windows, its towers and minarets
dominating Nork. It extended from what seemed the ridge of
the lowest part of the island clear to the river's edge, where a
strong keep guarded the near end of the bridge and admitted
those entering the city through a fortified archway.

I stared about me with dawning recognition, and suddenly

sank down among the stones, crushed with horror. I covered
my face with my hands to shut out the sight. For that on which
I looked had been New York.

The ruins on which I stood represented the remnants of the
tall buildings of what had been Park Row.

This was no past age into which I had strayed, but one that
would not dawn for many merciful centuries. Chandra had
carried me very far from the age of the Vikings!

Presently I gathered strength to look about me again: at the
low houses of stone, perched so high above the streets beneath,
and then upward where, story on story, in tier on tier of splendid architecture, Og's palace rose, the wonder of the world, and
erected, too, by builders of a vanished day. From within it came
one sound, thin as the whir of grasshoppers, and yet as insistent;
the shrilling of the fifes.

The thought of the descendants of these great builders,
herding, wretched slaves, among the ruins, overwhelmed me.
But then I thought of Alma, wailing for me, for my deliverance;
and I rose, strengthened.

I moved down a path among the debris, toward the main
road of the city, which led to the gates of the palace. I passed
the booths of the marketmen, where the head of the bridge
caravan had already halted, the drivers unloading bales of mer-
chandise and produce from the backs of their beasts. Lines of
slaughter-camels stood patiently in row before the closed butch-
ers' shops. Beyond I saw strange smacks, heavy with fish, lan-
teen-sailed, careening into port or skimming the waters of the
wide bay.

A few of the Yuki, attired in black, like myself, were lurching
homeward from the great feast which had been free to all,
within the palace court. The great bronze gates stood open wide
before me. The bowmen, guarding the entrance, did not molest
me. I looked to them like any Yuki.

Then my memories of the past, awakened for the nonce by
the shock of my discovery, grew dim again. I knew myself only

for the swineherd's boy who had come to Nork to see his destiny; and I went in.

The court was enormous, and everywhere the Yuki had been feasting around innumerable camp-fires. I passed lines of tethered camels, palanquin-bearers, asleep beside their loads, waiting for their lord's return from the revels in Og's famous hall above. Men and beasts were scattered promiscuously about the flags, yet so huge was the court that vast spaces of it were empty. Here and there stood the guard, armed with long yataghans.

I passed among a few of the revelers, bound for their homes, and went toward the center, attracted by what I saw. Around the court ran a high roof, set upon pillars of chalcedony, above which, at the far end, I saw the trunks of the trees of Og's pleasure-garden, raised high above the ruins upon a hundred columns. The roof was built about a gigantic bronze statue of Buddha, of which my foster-father had often told me, green from the weather; for the roof had been left open about it, to accommodate the gigantic idol, which was only visible from the navel downward.

Standing beside this image, I looked up to see the great body towering above. I discovered that the statue was hollow; through chinks in the casting I could glimpse the white interior walls, red from the reflected fires below.

Immediately above the roof was the rotunda of the belly, which I had seen from the pit. Round and about the image ran a spiral stairway of black stone, guarded by five Yuki swordsmen.

Suddenly there sounded the blare of trumpets at the gates, and the few who moved inside the court flung themselves to the ground, leaving me standing. In rode Prince Timour, accompanied by his retainers.

After the all-night carousal he had been hawking upon the marshes by the seashore. A hooded bird perched on his wrist, and as his horse moved the tiny bells upon the jesses tinkled melodiously.

The glances that Timour cast to left and right out of his keen, black eyes were as bright as the eyes of his bird beneath the half-lifted hood.

The great prince was a hideous figure, and yet not altogether unpleasing to the sight, if only from the air of power and manhood that radiated from him. Short, compact, and of immense muscular strength, he sat on his horse like a centaur, riding with stirrups so short that the saddle might have been a chair. His agate spurs hardly reached to his horse's flanks. A wisp of black mustache coated his lip. His yellow face expressed determination, cruelty, and fearlessness, with consciousness of power.

As he rode in I saw a band of priests, robed in yellow garments woven of camel's wool, descend the stairs of black stone. Preceding them came two girls, fifing with distended cheeks.

"Hail, Timour!" they saluted him. "Already the hour of sacrifice approaches; hot burn the fires, but no victim is nigh."

Timour reined in his horse abruptly, so that it sat back on its haunches, and glared about him.

It was an inauspicious salutation, and he knew it well; for the lack of a victim for the priestly sacrifice was an event dreaded by the superstitious Yuki.

His glance fell on me, standing alone among the prostrate multitude. He stood up in his short stirrups, seeming to pull the horse to its feet by sheer power of his arms.

"Down, dog, when Timour rides!" he cried; and, straight as an arrow, the uncoiling lash-tip leaped toward me and flicked me across the face. The leaden pellet at the end of the thong hit deep into the skin. I felt the blood start.

The shock of the blow sent me reeling backward, but only for an instant. Mad with fury, I sprang forward, caught the whip, wrenched it from Timour's hands, and raised it on high.

Before it could descend his followers had leaped from their horses and seized me. They looked for their leader's signal.

Timour scowled savagely and wrenched his long yataghan from its scabbard. Twice it swept through the air, halting each time within an inch of my throat. For the third time Timour drew back the blade; then he lowered the point and replaced it in the scabbard.

"Ho, Epsilon!" he called to the chief priest above. "Here is your sacrifice, that there need be no hunger in the Buddha's belly upon this day of good auspices."

CHAPTER VI

THE FOOD OF BUDDHA

WITH YELLS OF joy the Yuki clustered about me, until I found myself the center of a vast throng, collected as if by magic, which almost filled the great court. The retainers of Timour, ringing me around, waited for the arrival of Epsilon and his band of priests, who, descending the stairs, came up to me.

"Thou knowest, O great Prince Timour, that it is not lawful to sacrifice one of the Yuki, unless he be a stranger from one of the tributary provinces," said Epsilon, eying me regretfully. "Whence do you come, O stranger, and what is your birth, that you may claim this honor?" he continued to me.

"I am from a far-away region by the seashore," I began, "but as for the honor, I do not desire it. I am on my way to seek audience of the king."

I had got thus far when I heard shouts behind me, and saw a little company of armed men spurring their way through the throng toward me.

"It is Ruuf, the king's son!" shouted the young man who rode at their head. "Deliver him to us, Epsilon, for such was King Og's demand, and we are his messengers."

I recognized the speaker as Halkh, the young noble who had been sent on the mission to bring me to the court. And, as I set eyes on his face, my wavering memory came back to me.

I recalled the robbers' ambuscade, which had scattered my guards by night, my attempts to rejoin them in the darkness, and the hot pursuit that had impelled me to take shelter among the ruins, where I had come upon the tunnel.

Timour's face grew dark.

"Seize him, Epsilon!" he shouted. "No doubt these are companions of this low fellow, planning to rescue him. You know the king's statutes," he added, "which command that, when there is a dearth of sacrifices, strangers are to be admitted to the banquet of the Buddha."

He nodded to his guards, who flung themselves in the way of my rescuers. I heard the clank of armor and the sounds of the scuffle as the two parties met. The unarmed Yuki fled in panic before this clash of the knights, while Epsilon and his priests, who needed no further instructions, seized me and, despite my struggles, carried me toward the idol.

I heard the creak of pulleys within the hollow figure, and suddenly, with a clang, a plate in the monster's foot fell to the length of its supporting chain, disclosing a sort of wicker cradle. Instantly I was forced into it, the plate rose up, cutting me off from the hall, and I swung at the end of a long cable of steel inside the Buddha.

Slowly, with a succession of jerks, the basket ascended. It swung from side to side of the great well, and the white walls seemed to circle round me as I clung dizzily to my precarious support. Far underneath me I could see the furnace fires, whose heat rushed up and smothered me in choking waves. Above me was the rotunda, like a huge bell, open at the top. As I neared this I could see the figures of the slaves upon the ledge, apparently working at the mechanism that controlled the moving basket.

Round and round the circular ledge of the Buddha's belly moved the tiny figures, laboring as if they were operating some windlass bigger than any ever fashioned by man before.

Had the basket descended, to cast me into the pit, I could have understood what my fate was to be; but I could not understand why I was being elevated toward the idol's belly, then above it, until the slaves beneath me were no larger than dolls; higher still, until I saw the interior of the dome of the head above me, and, high above that, the beams supporting the minaret which was the brain.

Suddenly the creak of the pulleys ceased, the basket jerked, hung motionless a moment, and then slid out of the hollow well laterally along a narrow passage. Simultaneously I heard the jar of some descending mass behind me, but I could see nothing in the darkness, and the reflection of the furnace fires no longer lit the interior of the cavern.

And then I found myself upon my feet in utter darkness, released from the tilting cradle, which was drawn upward by the ropes toward the minaret.

I stood still, too helpless to attempt to fly, too ignorant of my surroundings to dare take one step forward or sideward. Behind me was the great hollow of the well. But under my feet was the firm structure of a floor.

I stretched out my hands before me, groping for something to take hold of. They encountered a gate, or door, of solid metal. I felt to the right and left. My hands touched the edges of the stone walls, into which the gate was fastened.

And suddenly, almost noiselessly, the gate was lifted.

The shock of light stunned me, the sound of innumerable voices rang in my ears. I found myself facing a multitude.

I was standing in the corridor corresponding to the Buddha's throat, between the lips and the palate.

On either side of me was a wall of masonry; nor could I imagine how I had entered that *cul-de-sac*, for behind me was an interlocking wall of white stone pillars, through which it would have been impossible for a cat to squeeze. In front of me the upraised metal gate hung from the beams overhead, leaving a grille or lattice work of strong steel bars, which effectively imprisoned me.

I stood in this cage at the end of a great hall corresponding to that beneath, and packed with a mob of black-clad Yuki, whom I could see still swarming in at the far entrance to the palace upon the upper level. As the gate rose they cheered and hooted, as if spectators at a play. And the thousands of eyes, each fixed on mine, contained neither pity nor anything but fanatical interest in what was to happen.

BEFORE the crowd, their bodies turned toward me, a band of yellow-robed priests was hymning a votive chant. And even above the droning prayers and the shouts of the mob rose the shrilling of the fifes from somewhere near me.

It was the daily sacrifice to the Buddha, made during certain seasons, when war captives or strangers from distant regions were to be obtained; and I was the sacrifice. I had heard of the rite from my foster-father, and accepted it as a part of the ceremonial of the faith, with hardly another thought. Whether my supporters had given up the attempt to rescue me, or had been beaten back, I could not know, but there was no friend in that vast audience. Beside the doors leading to the stone stairway I saw Timour, standing amid his retainers.

As the shouting that had greeted my appearance died away, he spoke to old Epsilon.

"Why is the sacrifice delayed?" he asked.

"We wait for our king, O Prince Timour," said the old man.

"Wait no longer, for he will not attend to-day," returned the prince. "Og sleeps on his throne after the festivities. Therefore proceed with the sacrifice, that our journey hither may have a propitious ending."

I glanced about me helplessly as Epsilon and his band of attendant priests drew near. Surely my journey was not to end in that rat-trap! I meant to fight, at any rate; but I could not discern whence the threatened death would come, unless through the cumbersome machinery of the Buddha's interior. There was no sign of knife or ax on Epsilon as he approached me.

"Take courage, O stranger!" he said to me. "To few is given the honor of becoming food for the Buddha, and thus bringing his gifts and bounty to the Yuki nation. But if, in ignorance, you fear to die, and do not know the true teaching of the Path, learn that death is nothing, for even as the caterpillar, having come to the end of his leaf, reaches out to another, so man, having put off his body, takes to himself another body. Therefore give thanks, O stranger, in hymn and praise, that this favor is accorded you."

Fine phrases for one in my situation! Before I could answer, the hidden fifes shrilled out so loudly that it would have drowned the cries of any anguished victim.

Simultaneously the populace began chanting a votive hymn, a savage paean that set the hall ringing. Their eager eyes were fixed on me. Timour, striding forward, ranged himself beside Epsilon and eyed me fiercely, as if he wished to glut his revenge for my resentment of his blow.

But suddenly, as he watched me, a curious look came over his face. He seemed as a man who has received some stunning revelation. He strode forward until he was standing against the grille, so close to me that we could have touched each other. As I met his gaze I was aware of an enmity that had existed, as my love for Alma had existed, through eons past.

Above the sound of the fifes and the chant of the priests and people I could hear Timour's hissing words:

"Where have I known thee? Speak!"

Before I could make answer, if there was any to make, I heard once more the clanking of the machinery that had drawn up the basket from beneath. And then the whole floor on which I stood quivered beneath me.

Suddenly, as I glanced backward, I perceived that the pillars of white stone were moving. More than that, I realized with numb horror that they were meant to be the representation of the teeth of the idol. In the light of the hall they were revealed to me in two serried rows, horribly chiseled to represent incisors and molars. The cracks that time had placed in them gave a further verisimilitude to the devilish work.

Each pillar was about twelve feet in height, and set into a stout socket of bronze, below which was an edging of red carpet, like a gum.

The upper row, descending from an iron base set fast in the roof, fitted into the interstices of the lower set, so that the whole formed an impenetrable barrier. Behind this I saw the red tongue of the monster, coiled in the throat by means of a strong steel spring on either side.

And it could only have been through that passage that I had entered the Buddha's mouth.

And through that passage I was destined to go; for the stone teeth of the Buddha were in motion.

The huge incisors and molars were beginning to grind laterally upon each other, the movement, whether designedly or not I do not know, producing the most intolerable grinding sound imaginable. It was that squeak, as of a pencil on a child's slate, that sets one's teeth on edge—but infinitely magnified and in itself an almost intolerable torture.

And the roof and the floor were the upper and lower jawbones!

For, as the teeth ground, the floor on which I stood went sliding backward and forth, while I clung to the walls and tried to steady myself. I could see Timour's face through the grille, peering into mine, with a look on it of devilish and barbarous triumph.

Then the whole floor went sliding forward, and simultaneously the shrilling of the fifes grew wilder, until the sounds seemed like needle-points against my eardrums.

Sliding, staggering toward the grinding teeth, I saw the steel springs uncoil, and the tongue of the Buddha came writhing through the air toward me. I stumbled, grasped it, clung to it, and poised myself upon it, with yawning emptiness beneath my feet as the floor of the passage tilted with the opening of the jaws, which now began to gnash in rhythm with the clanking of the machinery that controlled the Buddha's movements.

Behind the opening of the jaws I saw the white walls of the well, red as the fauces of a throat now, from the reflection of the leaping fires below.

And I saw my fate, imminent before me. For, wide though the jaws of the monster idol opened, they did not open so wide that I could plunge through to a quick and merciful death. I saw how the monster stones would seize me and press the life out of me, and grind me fine before hurling me in fragments into the fires below.

The tongue was a soft, furry mass about six feet in width at the tip, but widening toward the base. It had the pile or nap of a carpet, and seemed to be woven of camel's hair, stained red, and laid upon a metal basis. As I bestrode it the tip began to curl upward and inward. I found myself sliding down toward the teeth beyond, which gnashed with fury. Another moment, and the trap would catch and hold me. I closed my eyes, I heard the shriek of the fifes, and caught a last glimpse of Timour, against the grille, and the faces of the multitude behind him, between the fringes of my eyelashes.

Then a sudden impulse made me open them. Within the passage, pressed close against the wall, and hidden from the sight of those outside the grille by the projecting rim of the masonry, I saw Alma.

CHAPTER VII

BEHIND THE CARPET

SHE STOOD LIKE any statue, and her eyes were fixed on mine in horror. As I clung to the Buddha's tongue, seeing the grinding stones before me, she pointed wildly and vehemently toward the wall.

In that instant I perceived that a narrow edge on either side of the floor had not swung downward, nor moved, as the rest moved. It formed the framework of the chamber, the supporting portion from which the floor was suspended, either on chains or hinges. It was, perhaps, a foot in width, and it was on this precarious platform that Alma was standing.

Instantly, instinctively, I poised myself in the hollow of the Buddha's tongue, and as it raised itself to fling me against the teeth I sprang.

Simultaneously the tongue-tip struck the moving stones, and, released of its burden, rushed back by the contraction of its springs into its place, while the teeth grated furiously and suddenly snapped fast.

Once more the end of the chamber was shut off by the still pillars of stone.

My leap carried me against the wall. I staggered and reeled backward. Alma put out her hands and pulled me to my feet. At the same time she caught my arm and extended it in front of me. I felt emptiness where the wall had been.

I perceived now a low doorway of stone, set so skillfully into the stone wall that I should never have perceived it.

For a moment I heard the sounds of the multitude within the great hall hushed, and only the shrilling of the fifes went on. Then roars of execration burst out, and the whole mob came surging forward.

I knew that neither Timour nor any of those within the hall had seen Alma, nor, indeed, did they know what had become of me, save that in some mysterious manner I had escaped the teeth of the Buddha. I heard the mechanism begin to clank, and guessed that in a moment the grille would open. I heard Timour's shouts of rage and the high treble of old Epsilon. But Alma had pulled me through the door and closed it. I heard the lock snap; and then we two stood panting and breathless behind it, cut off from every sound without.

"It is a secret way, built by Og when he feared for his throne," gasped the girl. "He told me the clue to it one night when he was drunk, and gave me the key from his girdle. I preserved it, thinking that some day I might have need of it; but I never guessed how much. Come with me!"

"Where do we go?" I gasped.

"We must go to King Og. It is our only chance, for all the exits from the palace are known. Our only hope is to reach the audience-hall before Timour and his band. Once there, I will kneel before King Og and plead for your life. He is merry when he has been drinking, and perchance will not refuse me."

I noticed that she spoke of the Yuki king as if he were some abstraction, something impersonal, which dealt out fate.

She took my hand and hurried me down a flight of stone steps in utter darkness. We entered a stone corridor, traversed it, passed through a doorway, and entered another hall, all in the same complete obscurity. It was an eery sensation, accompanying the girl through these hidden mazes of the great palace, like rat-runs, so closely were the heavy walls set together; yet, though we seemed remote from all other human beings, I felt their presence behind those walls, as a spider in its web feels what is passing. The whole, old evil place might have been telling of its secrets, its crimes, its shames, and sorrows.

We passed through another doorway, and now we began to hear once more a faint but unmistakable sound. It was the hammering of the armorers in the pit. And we emerged upon the great well, with its white walls, once more.

Alma uttered a cry, stepped back, and pointed. I saw that the lower part of the flight of steps, which had run almost vertically down the side of the well, was gone. A great fissure showed where the broken structure had fallen, to swell the heap of ruins in the pit far beneath us.

There seemed no possibility of continuing our journey. Alma looked at me hopelessly.

"We must go back," she whispered. "It may be that we can reach the audience-hall by other ways. There are many corridors that run through the palace. If we wait until nightfall, perchance Timour's watch will be relaxed—"

She ceased, for at that moment we both heard, far away, the crash of masonry and the distant shouts of the Yuki. And as we crouched there, listening, we heard the voices of our pursuers, far away through the corridors, but drawing nearer, and mingled with the tramp of steel-shod feet on stone.

There was no need to inquire what had happened. Timour had discovered the secret entrance and battered down the bolts of the door.

We were trapped helplessly. I glanced about me for any desperate means of escape, and I saw one barest chance for us.

The lowest step of the flight on which we stood was about forty feet above the belly of the Buddha, the spherical protuberance ringed with the circular platform on which the slaves were laboring. The broken flight had led down to this platform, for the lower exit was visible, a dark opening in the wall of the shaft.

The mechanism that had opened the Buddha's jaws had, at the same time, lowered the cable that held the cradle, to receive its next victim. The rope oscillated between the walls of the central well. As it swung toward me, I leaped.

It was a mad leap from a standing posture, and failure would have precipitated me into the fires beneath. But I caught the cable, and clung to it with bleeding hands, and, swinging thus, endeavored to increase and direct the oscillation toward Alma, who crouched on the stair gazing at me in terror.

Even as I hung there I heard the pursuit quicken. The voices of the Yuki could be heard plainly. Each moment I expected to see them appear at the head of the broken stairway.

Slowly, very slowly, the long pendulum of steel increased its strides. Now it swung almost from wall to wall. I measured the distance, I clung with one hand, and, bending, caught Alma about the waist and pulled her to me with an exercise of strength that now seems incredible to me. Then, supporting her with one arm as she lay limp against the cable, I made my swift descent.

I had seen that the twoscore slaves upon the circular platform were operating the mechanism that controlled the jaws. I had discerned a number of levers attached to a moving rail in such a manner that each slave, after a certain number of pulls, completed the circuit of the platform. Round and round went the toiling figures, paying not the least attention to me as I hung opposite the belly of the idol.

I waited till the moment of inertia at the end of the swing and flung out my legs, grappling one of the levers. The return impetus of the steel cable tore the skin from my calves, but I held against the pull of the chain till it hung loose beside me, and, straddling the lever, waited to catch breath and restore the numbness of my arms. The slave attendant upon the lever, who did not seem to understand the nature of my intrusion, tried to pull it down, and meeting the lower part of my body abandoned the attempt, and stood waiting beside the machine.

His stoppage arrested the progress of the next, and in a minute the whole docile twenty-four were motionless at their posts.

Then I realized that these men were blind from the darkness

and deaf from the constant clank of the mechanism. Not a head was turned toward me as I sat there.

Suddenly the yells burst out overhead. The Yuki had found the stairway. Instantly, before we were seen, I leaped to the circular platform, gained the recess, and set Alma down beside me.

The circle of yoked slaves, patient as cattle, cowered at the brush of our bodies, as if fearing the lash. The sight roused my indignation and nerved me to the difficult enterprise.

I held Alma in my arms till she had regained her power of movement, shrinking within the opening in the wall, while overhead the baffled Yuki chattered excitedly and peered down into the pit, at the bottom of which they thought we lay.

It was hardly a moment before Alma struggled out of my arms.

"Come, Ruuf!" she gasped.

Hand in hand, we raced once more through the blackness of secret passages. We climbed interminable flights of stairs. I had no idea of the topography of the place, but once, seeing through a chink in the wall the dull reflection of fires, I inferred that this was an inner stairway that ran parallel to the outer one of black stone that wound about the body of the Buddha.

At last we halted for an instant and I caught at my breath. I heard Alma pant at my side.

"Farewell, Ruuf!" she whispered. "I can do no more now; and yet perchance we shall meet soon. Pass under the carpet at the end of the corridor."

She stooped and pressed a catch. A door swung open. I stepped forward and it closed behind me.

At once the shrilling of the fifes, which had been inaudible, burst forth again.

I found myself in a corridor of the palace, which was filled with divans on which armed guards were stretched out in drunken slumber. Black pages at the doors slept bolt upright.

I looked to the right and left. To the right I saw the upper levels of the ruins, and a great door that opened into the corridor immediately from the street without.

On the left was a hanging carpet concealing the entrance to a hall or room. From this direction came the sound of the fifes, now very near.

Hardly had I entered the corridor than shouts came from the street without. The sleeping guards struggled to their feet, instinctively feeling for the yataghans beside them. Three horsemen came galloping through the entrance, spurring their horses right along the corridor. At their head was Timour upon a milk-white steed.

Behind them I heard the gallop of other horse-hoofs and other cries.

I ran to the end of the hall, pushed aside the hanging carpet, and found myself in a small chamber in which stood twenty female fife-players, as motionless as statues save for the movements of their hands and their distended cheeks. My entrance did not disturb them. They played as they had been trained to do, for they were all deaf and blind, like the pit-slaves but, unlike them, from birth.

I ran past them, hearing my pursuers clattering behind me, pushed aside a second carpet, richly woven and dyed in amber and black, and found myself in the great audience chamber of King Og.

CHAPTER VIII

OG, THE KING

THE HALL WAS filled, but among that whole multitude only two men were awake. The rest, extended on the rugs that covered the floor, were snoring loudly, their yataghans beside them, exhausted from the drinking and the revelry of the night that was gone.

Along the walls were ranged tables of precious woods, inlaid, containing remnants of a Gargantuan feast in the shape of half-sodden joints and demijohns of porcelain, which, overturning, had poured their contents upon the rich rugs on the floor. Huge vats of rice-wine stood against the walls. An entire camel's head, stuffed with herbs, leered at me from a golden dish.

Squatting upon her haunches at the far end of the hall, King Og's mare, trained to immobility, watched for her master's waking.

Og slept upon his golden throne beneath a canopy of silk. He was clad in a wine-stained robe of iridescent yellow, and the gold crown on his head, slightly awry, disclosed the bald head beneath. A thin beard of snowy white fell over the great heaving chest.

His right hand, holding the unsheathed sword which he must never lay aside, was upheld by one of the two retainers who were awake. The second man supported his left arm. Thus held, since the laws of the Yuki forbade their ruler to lie down to sleep, Og slumbered.

To my surprise I saw the passage leading into the Buddha's

mouth behind the throne. A bulge in the wall indicated the face. The two eyes were windows high in the wall behind the throne of gold.

I ran forward, hearing the pursuing horsemen ride into the room of the fife-players. After them came others, yelling and slashing their yataghans through the air. As I entered there came a blast of horns from the minaret overhead, and instantly, as if by magic, the whole court was awake and on its feet.

King Og yawned mightily and sat upright. I flung myself in supplication upon the steps of the throne, just as the group of horsemen came full gallop along the hall and clustered about me, Timour at their head, eying me like tigers.

But after them came others; and now, raising my eyes, I saw Halkh and his three supporters ranged between myself and Timour; and all looked toward the throne, where Og was still yawning.

In the hush that followed, Og spoke, and his voice was a bellow almost as loud as the echoing reverberations of the horns, drowning the squeaking fifes without.

"What is this, Prince Timour, that you disturb my slumbers?" roared the king. "Am I the ruler of the Yuki, and shall I not sleep in peace when I am drunk?"

"Look on me, O king!" cried Timour, vaulting from his horse, which immediately crouched low upon the floor. He strutted forward on his short legs and shook his fist. "This madman has dared to raise his hand against me; yea, more, he has escaped by magical arts from the throat of the Buddha in which he had been honored. Say the word that shall consign him to torture."

"Is that all you have awakened me for?" grumbled the sleepy monarch. "Take him to the torture, then, and turn me on my right hip, so that I may stretch myself."

They leaped toward me, but Halkh sprang from his horse and held out his hands toward the king in supplication.

"This is your son, Ruuf, O king, to fetch whom you sent me to the far regions by the sea!" he cried. "Lo, robbers attacked us, and in the darkness we were scattered, so that we could not find your son, Ruuf, until even now in the palace. By the ring that is on his finger I claim your protection, O king!"

I stretched out my finger, on which the great ruby scintillated.

King Og uttered a cry, rose from his throne, and tottered down the steps, supported by his two retainers. The old man was between six and a half and seven feet high and built like a barrel. He placed one enormous hand behind my shoulder and swung me about, peering into my face.

"He has his mother's look," he mumbled.

At this scene Timour drew back, looking as black as thunder. His followers, who had dismounted, grouped themselves about him, rattling their half-drawn swords ominously.

"It is false. He is an impostor who has possessed himself of the ring, O king!" said Timour fiercely. "Should the true son of Og raise his hand against Og's ally, Timour? Nay; and should Og's son flee in the night from thieves?"

"Thieves led by Timour's men!" cried Halkh hotly. "Does the great Timour so fear thy son, O king, that he seeks his murder by the wayside?"

"I do not know," answered Og. "Wise though my judgments be, they are not rashly given. In my 'Book of Wisdom' I have written. 'Read not men by their follies, but by the superabundance of their words.' However, I am beginning to wake up now, and feel inclined to let this matter be tried. So summon hither the Princess Kara, being Ruuf's betrothed, and she shall decide, for the promptings of a woman's heart are inspired by the holy Buddha and do not err."

At his words a loud shout of applause rang through the court.

"Truly, O king, thy judgment are marvelous," murmured old Epsilon in the king's ear.

The old scoundrel stood there at Og's side, purring in the sunshine of the royal presence and eying me with a smile that betokened something else than benevolence.

"And let the Princess Alma attend also," continued Og, "in order that her counsel may aid her sister's, for I have written in my 'Book of Wise Proverbs,' 'Although the words of women be like water, yet, if a woman and her sister are in agreement, let the wise men accept their counsels.'"

He stroked his great stomach reflectively and shuffled back to his throne, while the courtiers muttered and the fifes went on without.

Presently a door clanged in the corridor, the carpet was pushed aside, and sixteen young women came in. All were dressed alike in billowy silk, fourteen had their hair pinned up with combs of lapis lazuli; but the two foremast wore golden coronets, and one of them was Alma, walking as serenely as if she had never participated in the events of that morning.

Beside her walked Kara, her half-sister; and never have I seen such contrast in two of the same blood. For Alma was fair as the dawn, and Kara dark as night. Alma's face was innocent and sweet, and her eyes looked out frankly upon the courtier, inclining toward her like marionettes. But Kara's dark eyes seemed to veil slumberous passions in their depths, the red flush on her olive cheeks lent her a radiant beauty, and yet her face was hard and the expression inscrutable. There was pride there, and cruelty; great love and greater hate could find their lodgment in her heart, I guessed.

The two women advanced to the steps of the throne and bent their heads before Og.

"This is my son, Ruuf, your betrothed, Princess Kara," grumbled the old king, patting my head with a huge hand. "He has shown me his mother's ring in proof of it; but Timour here says he is an impostor. So we'll leave the decision to you, and if you and the Princess Alma agree, no doubt it will be right. Be quick, in order that we may begin our feasting again."

The Princess Kara stood still before me, scanning my face. My life hung, I realized, upon this woman's whim, and I knew that her whim would suffice her for her decision.

For minutes, as it seemed, she watched me. I felt that the impression I made was neutral. My eyes shifted to Alma's face. Quick as a flash I saw Kara look at her half-sister also. It was but a flicker of the eyelashes, and yet in that moment Kara saw the agony of the suspense, and guessed at what she did not know.

I saw an angry color mantle Kara's cheek, and then a smile began to spread across her mouth.

"It is not meet that a woman should dare to offer judgment in your presence, O great Og," she answered. "Therefore, in accordance with your statutes, let the matter be tested by the Trial of the Mares."

I saw Timour nod and blink in gratification; old Og scowled morosely, and I suspected that Kara's judgment was an adverse one for me.

"Ah no, O king!" cried Alma quickly. "What chance of life will your son, Ruuf, have if he is matched against mighty Timour? Spare him and let him go!"

Her words created a sensation among the courtiers; I saw some look at their fellows and laugh, and look toward the princesses and laugh again.

"I was drunk when I wrote that statute," mumbled Og; "but a statute is a statute. Be it so, then!"

The animation among the men-at-arms increased. I perceived that a number of those who were grouped about Timour quietly shifted their position, clustering about myself, until two rival parties came into being before Og's throne. I inferred that an old feud existed between Timour and Og, and that my proposed marriage to Kara, and Timour's to the Princess Alma, had both been well-devised pieces of statecraft to uphold Og's kingdom.

King Og waved his hand. "Let it be as I have said!" he announced.

The courtiers instantly began trooping out of the hall and down a stairway that led from the anteroom in which the blind girls were filing. Og's roar arrested them; the entire court stood motionless, waiting upon his words.

"LET THE BLACK mare of Hanibeesh be brought," he cried, "since not even the best judges in my kingdom have been able to award the leadership to her or to the white mare of Timour. Ruuf, my son, if you are my son, which I believe, what do you say?"

"I am content, O king," I answered, understanding nothing of the proposition, but resolved to put a good face on my situation.

"Good!" he grunted. "If Timour conquers you, you are not my son, according to my statutes, and you go to the torture, or otherwise, as Timour wishes. If you win, I shall banish Timour from my kingdom and make war upon him. It is time there was war again, for my hand is growing slothful for want of use."

As he spoke I noticed that he caressed a large, bleached skull, from which he had been drinking, in an intimate and rather affectionate manner, and all at once it occurred to me that this bore, in its contours, a remarkable resemblance to Timour's close-cropped head.

"But I think you will be beaten, Ruuf, my son," continued the old king, "and I am sorry that I wrote that statute. No man in the five kingdoms has ever thrown Timour, Prince of the Yuki, though no man ever had such a mare as Zora, of Hanibeesh. I shall be very drunk to-night after you are dead, for my heart yearns toward you. Drink before you fight to hearten you, and reflect that the man who once owned this head was a proper man, though foolish, and greatly esteemed for his skill in battle. He was Timour's father."

He held out the grinning skull, brimful of rice-wine, to me; but I could not overcome my repugnance at sealing my lips to such a cup. Og saw me wince, and laughed.

"I am afraid that you are going to be overthrown," he said. "My heart aches for you, Ruuf, my son."

He waved his hand toward his courtiers, who at once began

trooping out, leaving the princesses and their attendants before Og's throne and a small body-guard of Og's personal retainers. Og nodded to one of these, who came forward. I noticed that his skin was fairer than those of the Yuki, and he bore a striking resemblance to the Princess Kara.

"Serve my son, Ruuf, to the trial," said Og.

The man came toward me and made a low obeisance. I noticed that he moved with a certain dignity, as of one born to rule; the expression on his face was captivating, but I read pride and self-will there.

"My lord, I am Tamsa of the royal line of Tamsa, and a kinsman of the princess," he said in a low voice. "I pledge my faith unto my lord till death."

We left the hall side by side, but I noticed that Halkh, who had never been far from me, looked angry for a moment, as if the newcomer had usurped his place. After us came the princesses and their women, and last the giant king, shuffling with his arms about the necks of his retainers.

Towering head and shoulders above the tallest of them, he looked a veritable Goliath. I could well believe that in his younger days he had been invincible; and, indeed, he had slain Timour's father, then regnant, in single combat, and thus acquired a throne, in accordance with the Yuki law of the royal succession.

We passed down the stairs and out into the royal garden.

It was a large tract of level ground, fringed with great trees and set on pillars above the court below. On a bed of masonry made from the ruins the turf had been laid deep enough to permit the centuries-old trees to strike roots and nourish. And, indeed, we might have been in an open field, save for the glimpse of the tall ruins on either hand beyond the trees, and the street cries, the tinkling camel-bells, and the great palace above.

At the side farthest from the Buddha, whose colossal outlines sent a long shadow across the grounds, was a black marble throne, with a smaller throne on either hand, and rows of black stone seats behind it.

The sound of the fifes swelled out, and the female fife-players came slowly into the grounds, followed by a band of soothsayers in their robes of yellow camel's wool. Following them came the princesses, and then Og with his body-guard.

But when Og took his seat, with Alma on his right hand, I noticed that the throne on his left was empty. The Princess Kara had stayed her journey at the far end of the grounds with Timour's men.

The act was so deliberate and unmistakable that the whole assembly hummed like a beehive and chattered excitedly, the Yuki stretching out their hands toward her and gesticulating.

The deliberate choice, or sponsorship, of Timour meant more than hostility to me, for Timour was the suitor for Alma's hand. So I interpreted it, and so did all the rest.

And I gathered from an almost imperceptible movement among the Yuki nobles that many of them would pledge their strength to Kara rather than to Alma.

The king half rose in his throne, took in the situation, and beckoned to me. I left Tamsa and Halkh, and the few who were grouped about me, and went toward the throne.

"Ruuf, my son," said the old king, "in my 'Book of Wise Sayings' I have written: 'Heed not the snake in the grass, for fear is on him. Heed not the hill-bear, for he is swifter in flight than thou. But heed the woman who hates, or she will bring thee low.' If thou canst conquer Timour, remember this, Ruuf, my son. Epsilon, my chief soothsayer, shall instruct thee in my wise teachings, if thou win in this contest."

"I shall remember, O king," I answered.

He grunted and turned away. I saw Alma's eyes fixed on mine in fear and pity, and the sight filled me with resolution to win.

Hastily I stepped to her side. "I shall conquer," I said, "for your sake, Alma, because you are for me, and not for Timour, for I love you."

She looked at me in consternation. A faint flush dyed her cheeks. She shrank away, and looking about me I saw that the whole field was watching me; my followers awaited me, and the stage was set for the battle.

CHAPTER IX

THE COMBAT

TWO OF THE black pages whom I had seen in the corridor of the palace were coming across the meadow, each leading a mare. One was coal-black, the other, Timour's, which I had seen, of snowy white. Both were wild and fiery creatures, with unclipped manes and tails that swept the grass as they moved forward, prancing and pulling at their halters. Each was shod with large shoes, and each appeared to be muzzled, though at the distance I could not be sure of that.

The white mare was led up to Timour. Wild as the creature seemed she crouched on the ground before him again, her ears laid back, her eyes rolling upon the black as she passed her, and the two neighed defiantly, as if they fully understood the part that they were to play.

As the black mare neared me I saw that her shoes were studded with formidable spikes, and what I had thought a muzzle was a contrivance with a hinge held by a strong, steel spring, and clamped to the jaws in such a way as to give the effect of steel teeth, which could be separated and snapped together with all the driving force of the jaw muscles behind.

The mare stopped of her own accord before me, whinnied, and crouched down as Timour's had done. She had neither saddle nor bridle. As I looked about me in perplexity—for I wondered with what I was to fight Timour—Halkh stepped quickly to my side.

He glanced apprehensively toward Tamsa, who was appar-

ently engaged in an altercation with Timour's second in regard
to the lie of the ground.

"Is my lord aware of the nature of the ordeal?" he asked in a
low voice, not meant to reach any ears but mine. And, stooping,
he made pretense of fastening my sandals.

"No," I replied.

He looked up at me in agitation. "The battle lies between
the mares," he said. "It is necessary only to retain your seat, for
he who first falls is beaten. Alas, had I but known this, my lord,
I would have fallen on Timour with my sword and died in your
place.

"Let me dare to speak quickly. If Timour wins he will assuredly take advantage of this strengthening of his ambitions to
challenge King Og to mortal combat, according to the Yuki
custom. And now that Og is old it is doubtful whether he or
Timour is stronger. Some day some chieftain will surely challenge him to gain the leadership, and Timour will not be
outdone.

"Let me speak on, my lord. I am one of those who have sworn
to set the Princess Alma upon her throne and free her people.
So is Tamsa, her kinsman; yet beware of him, for he has his
own ambitions. We had planned to revolt against King Og to
save the Princess from Timour. But if Timour be thrown that
matter must wait, for Og is old and plans to set the white people
free, though fear of Timour's power has held him back from it.
Therefore, if you win, my lord, we must support Og for the
present. Has my lord understood?

"Then let me speak once again. Half Yuki am I, even as my
lord; yet I have learned of his purpose to free the Princess Alma,
and I swear to be his true henchman henceforth, in life and
death. Does my lord trust me?"

I grasped his hand and nodded. Halkh rose and left me with
an obeisance. Og clapped his huge hands. There came a blast
of horns, the fifes shrilled loudly, and I had just bestridden my
mare, whose halter the black page had slipped, when she leaped

to her feet and pranced, head down, across the meadow to meet the white.

They stopped within a few feet of each other, whinnying defiance, and began to circle warily about each other.

I looked at Timour. He sat impassively upon his steed, his arms folded across his breast, his black eyes fixed on mine in mockery. There was a foretaste of victory in the smile upon his mouth. I looked from him to Kara as the line of his followers crossed my vision. She, too, smiled, and the look of disdainful anger upon her face made my former belief concerning her clear as daylight. She had enticed me into this predicament that I might make sport by my death at the expense of Alma.

I meant to win, with all that hinged upon the result. I was no longer afraid of Timour, novice though I was. And I realized that our riders' part, although apparently nothing, was actually the more important one. It consisted in that subtle and inexplicable communication of man to horse which adds his intelligence to beast's instinct.

It was the single feature in the game that, given an equality on the part of the mares, would bring victory. I realized this as my mare darted forward, so swiftly as almost to unseat me, the steel teeth drawn apart. But what fell short or wherein I failed her I do not know; only a moment afterward I had regained my seat to see Timour's smiling face before me again, and to hear the triumphant shouts of his supporters.

My mare's stride changed to a choppy gallop, as when a steed feels an indifferent horseman on its back. I pulled myself together and tried to will her to confidence in me. Suddenly, as a trout leaps from water, Timour's mare poised herself for an instant on the four hoofs drawn under her and sprang at mine. I heard the steel teeth snap viciously beside me.

She could have bitten deep into my leg, for I was completely surprised by the maneuver, and all but unseated me again. But evidently the animals were trained not to attack men. My black mare's deftness saved us. Again applause rang out, but this time it came from my men.

With a graceful bound my mare turned, and then so quickly and unexpectedly that I reeled a third time in the saddle, shot her spiked hoofs with terrific force into the while mare's flank.

The white went, staggering across the mead like a boy who loses his balance on a slide, recovered herself, and came forward viciously, shaking her head from side to side. She leaped, and mine, avoiding her once more, planted her hoofs in the same place again, this time ripping the flank and staining the white hair with blood.

Timour's mare upreared, shrieking, and brought down her sharp hoofs upon the shoulder of the black.

At the sight of the blood the crowd grew frantic. They broke from their places and came scrambling forward, forming an irregular circle about us. In vain the horn-blasts sounded in warning; it was quite clear that much more than a man's life hung upon the issue. I was the center of a political situation at which I could only guess; old hates, old rivalries stood out, naked as day, and the swords of the Yuki clansmen, half drawn from their scabbards, betokened bloodshed, whatever the issue.

Timour's mare began prancing ostentatiously at her success, but mine turned her head and looked at me in pitiful surprise. I saw that I had fallen short of guiding her in the ghastly sport, by a touch of the knee, or a hand's pressure upon the mane. I was as confused as she, and before either of us could recover confidence, Timour's animal had leaped again, and her teeth caught in the black's mane.

The wound was slight, but the steel teeth held like a trap, and the white mare, more powerful, though less agile than the black, shook mine and worried her. Round and round we spun, each animal making ineffectual parries and feints, while trying to reach the other with the spiked hoofs. Timour's grinning face was a dozen times within a hand's breadth of mine. With arms folded, he leered at my efforts to keep my balance. Alma, Og, whirled about me; now I faced the glum visages of my own men, now the grinning ones of Timour's; then, just as I was about to fall, the black mare broke away and bounded over the field, leaving a mouthful of hair between the teeth of the white.

She stopped, panting, with down-hanging head, blood streaming from her wounded shoulder. I laid my hand upon her neck and caressed her. It seemed to encourage her. She turned as Timour, convinced of victory, drove the white mare straight at us, with mouth wide open and steel teeth gaping.

My mare stood still until she was within a few feet, then wheeled and drove her hind legs into the belly of the white.

The white mare shrieked like a man under torture, and sprang backward a dozen paces. She quivered, she sank upon her haunches. I heard wild shouts break out from about Og's throne. I saw the leering mask of Timour's face alter to rage and surprise as he shot a lowering glance at me. He had accredited me with my mare's maneuver.

The courtiers thought so, too. I saw several of them leave Timour's body-guard and cross toward mine, convinced that he was beaten. Meanwhile the ring contracted, until the Yuki were almost within reach of the hoofs of the two animals, and the shouting was continuous.

Staggering and uncertain, Timour's mare came forward. And, just as I felt my black draw in her limbs, and thrill with the nervous preparation for the knock-out blow, the white dropped the play of weakness and shot forward like a dart.

Jaws open, teeth fringed with their horrid tips of steel, she rushed at us. The hot breath hissed on me, the protruding tongue brushed my leg. The teeth snapped fast in my mare's neck. She reared, upraised her forelegs, missed her air, and came down bestriding the white. With whinnies and grunts of fury the two creatures fought in the death grapple.

They worried each other like giant terriers, and the blood and sweat streamed down their hides. The courtiers ringed us, shrieking, the horns never ceased to blow, and above it all I heard the penetrating music of the fifes.

Then the white mare weakened and tore herself away.

I knew by the ghastly look on Timour's face that his animal was in sore straits. I clung to the black mare's mane, while, like a boxer, she measured the distance for her blow.

Then I saw Kara leave her followers and dart swiftly forward. I saw her for a moment stand at Timour's side—the next instant she seemed to have emerged from underneath my mare. And through the whirl of men I had an instant's vision of the girl thrusting a keen-pointed, needle-shaped dagger beneath her robe.

The next, my mare's forelegs had struck the white mare's flank, over the heart. Timour's steed reared, staggered, and plunging forward, flung him to earth.

A roar went up that deafened me. The yelling throng surged round me. But before they could acclaim me victor my mare whinnied, turned her head to look at me with agonized appeal in her bright eyes, and dropped like a stone.

CHAPTER X

THE DEFIANCE OF TIMOUR

I FELL BACK into Halkh's arms. I knew I was the victor, but by a scant quarter minute. Timour's mare lay panting upon the grass, but mine was stone dead, thrust through the heart by Kara's treacherous dagger. I knew it from the look of baffled hate upon Kara's face.

Timour had withdrawn a little distance, and, with arms folded, was glaring defiantly at King Og, whose men, their forces swollen by many of Timour's followers, still cheered for victory.

Then I saw Kara whispering in Timour's ear. He shook his head impatiently, but she continued, and presently I saw him mask the fury on his face with blandness.

He advanced toward Og, who sat upon his throne like a great idol in its shrine, his arms upheld by his two attendants, and his long yataghan pointed toward the defeated prince.

"Greetings, O king!" he called. "O king, great ruler of the city of Nork and the live tributary kingdoms, I have been overcome in fair contest by your lawful and true son, Prince Ruuf of the Yuki. You have threatened me with banishment and war. In my pride I have been abased, for who is strong enough to war upon Og and conquer?"

What scheme was hatching now, I wondered. Surely it hid some prize worth having to induce Timour to stoop to such appeal!

"There is none can war on me and conquer, for I am earth's greatest king," answered Og. "Speak on, Prince Timour!"

"But," Timour continued, "hawk does not war on hawk, though it has flapped its wings. Give me the Princess Alma in marriage, let your son Ruuf, my lord, take the Princess Kara, as she is willing; thus our feud shall be forgotten."

Og rose from his throne and towered above the soothsayers and the blind fife-players, whose shrill notes changed to a gentle melody.

"You have appealed to Og's mercy, Timour," said the king, "and Og of the Yuki is a clement ruler. But I am known as Og, the lawgiver, and a statute is a statute. The wise words that flow from my lips and are written down are alone greater than I. Let my son Ruuf decide, as is his right."

He turned toward me.

"Are you indeed willing to wed the Princess Kara, and accept Prince Timour into allegiance, Ruuf, my son?" he asked.

"I am not willing, O king," I answered. "I am not willing, for I know that the heart of the Princess Kara does not lie upon her lips, and that the same anger against her sister that would have sent me to my death is even now conspiring evil against me."

There was a silence of stupefaction following my words. Then Og threw back his mighty chest and laughed, and the sound of his laughter was like a score of brass instruments answering the fifes.

At their king's bellow all his followers took up the jest. The whole assemblage round about him rocked with laughter, while Timour's men, scowling, looked to their leader for a sign.

But before Timour could answer, Kara, who had grown flaming red, sprang forward, her breast heaving, her eyes flashing on me, on Og, on Alma.

"How long shall this insult go unavenged, O great king?" she cried. "Are you King Og of the Yuki, and shall you see your adopted daughter put to shame by a base impostor? He thinks to escape free after the insult that he has placed upon me, but he does not reckon with the vengeance that shall fall upon him!"

I thought this brazen challenge would precipitate a crisis, but Og sent forth his brass bellow again, and again his men answered him.

"In my wise books I have written," he said, " 'a woman's weapon lies between her teeth; strike her not, for her sword is sharper.' "

He turned to his chief soothsayer. "To-night, when I am drunk, read to me from my sayings, that I may delight in them," he commanded.

Timour strode forward until he stood face to face with the sacred fife-players, whom he dared not pass.

"Timour shall speak for Timour!" he cried. "Harken, O king!

"Shall Timour, then, be ousted from his lord's land like a dog, because this fellow, armed with the magic of old Malachi, has overthrown me? I swear no, by the brazen Buddha!

"Give me the white Princess Alma to be my handmaiden, and I will depart to my own people, and there shall be no war between King Og of the Yuki and Prince Timour, his servant."

All eyes were turned on Alma as the girl rose slowly out of her place beside King Og.

"Prince Timour," she answered, "great though you are, and mighty, had I a thousand lives I would give them freely rather than be handmaiden or wife; for I am of the royal line of Tamsa."

Timour glared furiously about him.

"Is it in your statutes, O king," he asked ironically, "that she on whom Prince Timour sets his heart shall refuse that honor, royal though she may be?"

King Og shook his head regretfully. "My statutes do not permit even a princess to refuse the honor of one of royal rank," he said. "I was drunk when I wrote that statute, but it cannot be changed."

With shouts of triumph Timour's men came running

forward. But I leaped between Timour and Alma, who stood speechless with fear before him.

"Hear me, O king!" I shouted.

"Speak, Ruuf, my son!" answered Og.

"I claim this girl, the Princess Alma, of the house of Tamsa, in place of the Princess Kara, as my right as of the royal line, and as Prince Timour's conqueror!" I cried.

The courtiers about me set up a shout that answered that of Timour's men. Timour stepped back, and his face was that of a snared wolf. Then Kara broke from out of the throng and ran toward me.

"This double insult that you have placed on me shall meet its reward," she cried. "I swear it. Is this the justice of King Og, the lawgiver? Aye, slink away, perjurer!" she continued, as I drew back before her fury. "But, though you may fly from me through the seven hells of Buddha, I will find you and bring you to judgment!"

Her words, her gestures struck some vibrating chord of memory. Somewhere, it seemed to me, I had stood in exactly the same place, and heard the same words from the Princess Kara's lips.

I stood before her, dazed. Presently, through the loud clamor that followed Kara's words, burst the rumble of Og's voice. He called to his chief soothsayer, who stood behind him writing in a parchment volume with a reed pen that he had drawn from his girdle.

"Let this be written in the 'Book of the Sayings of Og, the Lawgiver,'" he commanded. " 'No hell of Buddha burns so hot as the fury of a woman scorned.'"

Timour, who had been fretting and fuming among his men, now strode forward and addressed King Og once more.

"Twice, O great king, I have sought favors at your hands," he began blandly, "speaking words that were not in the heart. This third favor Timour asks, speaking truly. Think well, therefore, before refusing it, O king, for even Prince Timour, humble though he is, will not plead with his lord forever.

"You have heard of the sealed vial, handed down to the princesses of the base ant-people, the earth-dwellers, by their wise ancestors. So long ago this potent drug was fashioned that the very purpose of it has been forgotten. This much the wise men of the ant-people have told me.

"Yet this much is known; that, in time of imminent peril, when the fortunes of the existing princess are at their lowest ebb, she may drink the contents of this vial, and so escape her destiny. And the rumor hath it that the breaking of the vial and the swallowing of its contents confers immortality, together with some other magic which has been forgotten.

"Yet more, the legend goes that, with the breaking of the vial the Yuki Empire falleth. Now, O great king, it was my purpose to obtain this vial that made me suitor for the Princess Alma's hand. Therefore, let her be freed from the contract by payment of the vial, which I have sought so long in vain.

"Thus, holding it, I shall guard your empire till you are gathered to your fathers, and afterward, drinking of it, I shall become immortal and found a new empire that shall last forever. And let there be no war between us."

"If any one is going to rule this land forever, O Prince Timour, I think it will be I," bellowed Og angrily. "The princess hath the disposition of the vial, for my wise men have warned me never to seek it. And as for your promise of peace, think you that Og the lawgiver is not also Og the warrior?"

"You speak as a king speaks," answered Timour. "But there is one louder voice than a king's—aye, and its tooth is sharper than Og's reed pen," he added, half-drawing his yataghan. He turned toward Alma. "Give me this vial," he said, "and Timour will protect thee through all changes of fortune—and of kingship—that are to come."

"I may not, Timour," answered the girl. "Not though I were

in your power, to break or crush, could I be false to the charge that has been laid upon me."

"You have heard the answer," I interposed. "Now go!"

Timour opened his yellow lips and gaped at me. His eyes found mine, and a light of dawning recognition seemed to enter them. He wheeled upon me, and, speaking uncertainly, as if he hardly knew what he was saying, or who he was, uttered words that thrilled me with fear, as if I heard the voice of a man long dead in my ear.

"You fool!" he muttered in English. "Why didn't you give me that vial when you had it, and become my friend, as I warned you, Basil?"

The name struck home. Basil! When had my name been Basil? What was it that pressed in upon my brain like a dagger-thrust?

I had the impression, too, that the yellow face which snarled into mine should have been darker. And the face of Kara, beside that other's, seemed familiar as one's own face in a glass.

And then I knew them—both of them. For an instant the whole setting of the garden seemed unreality, and, like the outlines of a flat picture against the palace wall, I seemed to see the house surgeon's room in Moreland's hospital. It seemed to me as if, by an intense effort of will, I could succeed in refocusing my consciousness.

But there was no Alma in that long dead and distant world. Rather stay here with my beloved than return into that life which she could never enter till centuries had passed.

That resolution drove the memories from my brain. The picture faded. I was back in the garden, facing Timour, and he, too, seemed to have forgotten.

The prince turned toward the throne. "I, Timour, swear," he said, "that I am mightier than Og, and with my own hands can break him and tear asunder the book of his foolish statutes."

Og grinned, and, with a sudden gesture of defiance, raised

his horrid goblet, which he had been caressing, drained it, and, buffeting the fleshless cheek-bones, tossed it away.

It bounced down the steps of the throne, revolved upon the sward, and rolled, a white, grinning thing, to Timour's feet.

"If thou be minded, O Timour," bellowed the old king, "to execute the immemorial law of the Yuki, not made by me, and to overcome me in single combat, even as I overcame him who ruled before me, and now lies there and smiles upon thee, as one at peace. If thou be minded to achieve the kingship over Nork and the five tributary kingdoms—fight!"

And, shaking himself free from his henchmen, he rose and came waddling down the steps of his throne, brandishing a yataghan as long as a man.

"Come, O Timour," he roared, "that I may make of thee what I made of thy father, and have a new goblet! For thy father was a proper man, but always a little weak in the head, which impelled him to disobey my laws which I made when I was only a prince among the Yuki; and lo, even yesterday I discovered that the crack in his skull causes my liquor to leak!"

Seven feet in height, or nearly so, and thick as two of Timour's build, in spite of his slow gait Og seemed an invincible antagonist. The Yuki shrank away, and even Timour, hand on his yataghan hilt, hesitated.

All eyes were turned on Timour's sword, whose bright steel crept by inches from its sheath—and stayed.

For two of his captains, breaking through the throng about him, and catching him by the arms, talked eagerly to him. Then, slowly, Timour sheathed his weapon, and, with a gesture of defiance, strode from Og's presence, turning twice or three times in doubt, but in the end yielding.

More than half of the company flocked in his train, leaving our numbers pitiably few. Most of those who accompanied him were young men, eager to salute the rising star. Some of Og's guards swarmed forward, as if to challenge them, but a gesture from their leader stayed them.

We heard the rattling of the horse hoofs along the corridors of the palace. Presently there followed the clatter upon the broken stones of Nork of Timour's cavalcade, and the dull clamor of the astonished populace.

And from the palace windows we saw the file of Timour's men crossing the slender bridge that linked Nork with the tributary kingdom of Baruk-Halin, over which Timour ruled.

"They should have been stayed," I said, wondering why Timour had been permitted to leave the keep.

"Lord Ruuf, we are too few," answered a voice in my ear; and, turning, I perceived Halkh beside me.

"It is best thus," he continued, "for now the old rivalry between the Yuki leaders will be fought out; and afterward, it will be easier for our princess to regain her throne, O my lord," he continued, "there will be much bloodshed throughout this land; but, if her followers prove faithful, next year shall see the Princess Alma queen over Nork and the five tributary kingdoms."

CHAPTER XI

ALMA'S COUNSEL

THE NEXT WEEKS passed like a dream, for it was difficult for me to adjust myself to the great happiness that had befallen me, and my astonishing position as heir to the Yuki Empire.

I recall those weeks now only as a succession of pageants. Servile crowds of my own color, and Yuki chiefs, with fierce bearing, from all the outer districts of the empire, flocked into Nork to acclaim me at public festivals.

I was initiated into ceremonies and instructed in the complicated ritual of the Yuki court. I slept and awakened to the perpetual music of the fifes. I led processions to barbarous temples.

My first act was to insist on the discontinuance of the daily sacrifice. I do not know what prompted me to this, for I had been reared in the acceptance of this custom, and my past was quite forgotten. But I demanded this from Og, speaking out boldly in the great council hall; and, in spite of Epsilon's frenzied protests, I carried my point.

"If we feed not the Buddha, surely he will turn against us in his rage and give the empire to Timour," declaimed the old soothsayer.

"Many have been the Buddha's feasts," I answered. "Let him now grow lean for a while, and perchance my lord's fear shall be on him, and not the fear of the Buddha and his servants upon my lord Og," I answered.

King Og looked thunderous at this daring speech, yet it determined the issue in my favor, for I had skillfully played a card of statecraft.

Among the masses of the people who represented an earlier infiltration of the Asiatic-Indian element into the country, there had been the tradition of a mild and gentle Buddha, abhorring even the shedding of animal blood. The Yuki, the last of the migrant races, who had swept down upon the land only two centuries before, had adapted this tradition to their own savage rites; but it had never gained popular favor outside Nork, even among the Yuki stocks, while the preponderant masses of the whites had wholly rejected it. My foster-father had taught me much of the legendary traditions of the white peasantry, whose blood had mingled with that of the Yuki clans, and, while the sacrifices had never aroused any antagonism in my mind, these prejudices had insensibly affected me.

But Og's dilemma had been this. It had been decided, in council, that the time had come to set free the enslaved white populace and build the empire on a broader foundation. This measure was calculated to gain the favor of the masses; on the other hand, it meant the fierce opposition of the priestly caste, which had a good deal of power. My declaration, therefore, put the problem squarely before the king, and his decision, greeted with wild applause by many of the populace present, encountered glowering looks from the soothsayers and most of the nobles.

The decision was followed, as it had to be, by King Og's proclamation of freedom for the masses of the white people. Nork gave itself up to unbounded enthusiasm. In this Tamsa, the kinsman of the princesses, reveled. At a bound he became a popular leader.

It had been decided that he should raise a regiment of the whites to cooperate against Timour, who was reported to be collecting a huge army from all parts of Baruk-Halin, a thickly populated island of large extent, and cut off from Nork by the deep river that flowed between the two kingdoms from sea to sea.

All day and night the anvils rang in the pit, where the armorers, now slaves no longer, worked with a will. All sections of the populace were enthusiastic for the overthrow of Timour, with the exception of two. One of these was the priests, the other the principal nobles and their retainers, deeply offended by the enfranchisement of the whites, and almost as much so by the new privileges of the Yuki peasantry, from whom they were divided by centuries of feudal privileges.

Both these went sullenly about their business in those days; yet, since the current of popularity was with me, they were carried along with it perforce.

If I had ulterior plans of overthrowing Og, I veiled them from myself. Indeed, my time was too much occupied for me to be able to speculate upon such matters; and all my spare thoughts were for Alma.

I did not even know that she loved me, or whether she accepted me as her only refuge from Timour, or some other choice of the king's. I meant to speak to her that night at the banquet, and I recalled her look, her blushes in the garden, and placed a dozen different interpretations on them.

It was about three weeks after Timour's defiance that we learned he had assembled his forces in his capital; and since we now felt strong enough to inaugurate our campaign, we were resolved to anticipate Timour's attack.

It was the afternoon before the grand banquet that was to be held after the Yuki fashion in the council room, at which my betrothal to the Princess Alma was to be proclaimed. It was expected that this last stroke of statesmanship would consolidate the Yuki Empire and completely reconcile the whites to Og's lordship. A meeting was being held to discuss our plan of campaign.

Og, who had won his throne by personal prowess, innocent of strategical art, had refused contemptuously to take part in the deliberations.

"You are my son, O Ruuf!" he bellowed at me in his mighty voice. "Therefore deliberate with my generals; and, when your plans are made, take command of my forces; for I am too old to take the field, and have many wise sayings still to utter."

I was seated at the council table, on which was spread out a crude map of the island of Baruk-Halin. Timour's capital was a stronghold situated among the ruins not far across the river, but guarded by the precipitous heights which made a frontal attack almost impossible of achievement. Conversely, a direct attack upon the lower slopes of Nork was equally hopeless. Many a war had been waged during past centuries between the greater island and the smaller, but victory, when the two kingdoms were not in considerable disparity, had always depended on the element of surprise, or upon treachery.

The sole access by land was across the slender bridge connecting the two islands; each end was fortified by a powerful keep, in which a score of men could defy a thousand.

With me were Khom, the admiral of Og's navy; Tamsa, the commander of the white regiment, and Halkh, whom I had appointed my principal captain, as well as the leaders of the loyal Yuki clans, discountenanced and fuming under their supersession by myself and the head of an obscure principality.

However, in spite of much intrigue and misrepresentation, I had resolved that Halkh, whose loyalty was beyond doubt, should command my forces under me.

We numbered some six hundred fully armored men, who formed Og's standing army, together with two hundred brought in by the feudal chiefs, making eight hundred in all. Against these we reckoned that Timour could bring nearly twelve hundred. In addition, however, we had Tamsa's white regiment, nearly eight hundred strong, less heavily armored, but capable of doing useful work as auxiliaries, once the shock of battle was broken. On the whole it might have been said that our sixteen hundred were perhaps equal, as a fighting body, to Timour's twelve hundred homogeneously equipped warriors.

Each side possessed perhaps five hundred light cavalry; but in addition we had two hundred bowmen, drawn from Halkh's realm, the most famous archers of the age, and fanatically devoted to their leader, while Timour could muster half as many, of indifferent value, and a hundred slingers, of whom we had none.

The rival armies were thus fairly well matched, with a slight preponderance in our favor; but Timour had the advantage in ships. An island surrounded on three sides by open water. Baruk-Halin excelled in its fishermen, and possessed nearly twice our number of craft of all sizes, capable of being converted into war-vessels, which, if they could not hope to land sufficient men along our shores to gain a footing there, could at least divert our strength and compel us to split our army by retaining a force to protect our coast line.

This was the problem over which we had been puzzling. For manifestly it was impossible both to guard our shores with the fleet and, at the same time, to utilize it to transport our army over the arm of the sea beyond the rapids, which separated Og's domains from those of Timour.

"It is no use planning, O Ruuf," said one of the leaders of the loyal clans, flinging his arm angrily across the map. "In many wars have I served since my youth up, and never has Baruk-Halin invaded Nork, nor Nork Baruk-Halin, save when there was treachery, or when the navy of the one power had been crushed in a sea-battle. Hear, then, my counsel.

"Let Khom marshal his ships, carrying our entire armed force aboard them, and let us sail boldly across the river and give battle to Timour's vessels."

"And risk disaster," I interrupted.

"What then?" he asked with a sneer. "Is not the son of Og, who was powerful enough to escape the mighty Buddha—yea, and to thwart him strong enough to vanquish Timour?"

"That is my opinion, too!" cried Tamsa, springing up from the table. "We have debated this matter so long that we are becoming hopeless of success. Either that or make peace with Timour!"

"In no other way can we land on the Baruk-Halin shores!" cried one chief after another.

The verdict was overwhelmingly against me. Only Khom and Halkh sided with me—the former because he knew, as a seaman, the hopelessness of the proposal; the latter from loyalty. And yet I could not bring myself to accept the plan.

Here were we, with an army fully as strong as Timour's, and hopeful of victory, bound by our unfortunate naval inferiority to risk everything upon a sea fight.

Khom rose. He was a tall, bearded man, with but little of the Yuki in his face, grizzled hair, weather-tanned, wrinkled eyes, and the straight speech of the seaman.

"I am prepared to attempt the enterprise, if my lord Ruuf shall so direct," he said. "Yet, knowing that on the sea fortune is less fickle than upon land, I say it is madness to stake the fortunes of the state upon our little force of vessels. Let my lord decide," he ended, turning to me.

"And let my lord remember," said the chief who had spoken, with a meaning ring in his voice, "that the Yuki people look to his leadership, and that which war cements slothfulness dissolves."

Loud shouts of applause echoed his words. I looked about me helplessly. We were three against ten, and probably in a greater minority outside the council. And we could not remain on the defensive and content ourselves with awaiting Timour's stroke.

But before the shouting had died down the carpet before the entrance was pushed aside and the Princess Alma entered. She was alone, and she advanced without hesitation into the room, approaching the council table.

"My lords. I have awaited your decision anxiously in my apartments," she said, "and the sound of the shouting made me hopeful that at last it has been made. Therefore I have come to inquire of my lord Ruuf concerning it."

She stood beside me, looking into the flushed and angry faces of the Yuki leaders.

Then Tamsa, who had been silent hitherto, though manifestly against me, spoke.

"O princess," he said, "long we have debated, and even yet the decision lies even in the balance. For our lord Ruuf is not willing to put all to the test by such a bold assault on Timour's shores by land as shall give us the victory."

"Nor has he an alternative to offer," cried one of the Yuki.

As Alma looked at me in inquiry I sketched the situation briefly. "Too much is at stake," I said, "for me to wish to engage in such an unequal battle when our force is stronger on land than Timour's."

"My lords, I am but a woman," Alma answered, "and have no right, I think, to speak in the council hall. And yet there has come into my mind a plan by which Timour may yet be outwitted and driven in defeat before us."

Standing at my side, she faced the wondering Yuki chiefs, speaking with flushed face and heaving bosom.

"My lords, you know that never, since there was first war between Baruk-Halin and Nork, has the invader crossed by the bridge which unites the kingdoms, for so strong is the fortress that guards it on either side that such an enterprise has been considered madness. And in the keep at either end of the bridge a score of archers could keep a whole attacking army at bay, so long as they had arrows to shoot.

"Thus it is likely that, though the far end of the bridge be guarded, yet the watch is not kept as it should be kept in time of war.

"Now here is my plan. To-night and to-morrow night are moonless. In the dark of to-morrow, after sunset, let a herd of oxen be driven upon the bridge, with a belled cow at their head to lead them, and at the same time let Khom send a few of his tallest ships along beside the bridge, and let his seamen be instructed to set up a shout, as if our entire army were attacking.

"Then, in the darkness, panic will fall on Timour, and he will send large forces to hold the keep against our attack, and he will draw up his ships behind it, to guard their sally-port, that they be not cut off from it, and to aid in the defense.

"Meanwhile, under cover of darkness, Khom will have sent the bulk of his vessels creeping along the shore northward, to pass the rapids by the unguarded channel, carrying our whole forces, except some fifty archers and a score of guards, who will defend our end of the bridge.

"Thus, before the trick is discovered, you, my lord Ruuf, will have disembarked your army upon the flank of Timour's, on the Baruk-Halin shore, where victory will be assured to you. And if this plan be the weak wit of a woman, pardon me, but, if it be wise, I commend it to you."

She ceased, and the Yuki stared in amazement at her, and at one another. Then suddenly spontaneous shouts rang out, the Yuki chiefs cheered her to the echo, and came clustering about us both, kissing our hands in homage.

Wild enthusiasm seized upon all, sweeping away even those who had been bitterest against me.

"If such be the nature of our women, shall Timour's strength not prove as a reed?" cried Tamsa eagerly to Alma. "O princess, gladly shall I accept the charge of this enterprise, and who knows but that, if the keep be weakly held, I shall even capture it and gain much honor for you."

"O Tamsa, it was in my mind to give this charge to you," I interposed, "but your words have changed my purpose. For such rashness as yours can best serve us in the field at the head of your regiment, while Halkh shall hold the keep with fifty archers, and neither leave it nor go further than the commands I give him."

"Nay, lord, but my place is at your side!" cried Halkh, turning toward me eagerly. "Surely my lord will not keep me back from the battle when he goes out against Timour?"

"Gladly would I have you, Halkh," I answered, "but there is

need of your loyal archers here, to guard Nork and the princesses, and of you to hold their ardor in check by obedience to my command."

"Yea, but let thy servant speak, lord," he pleaded, drawing me a little aside from the Yuki, who, clustering about the princess, were not observing us. "Does not my lord see that discontent is rife among the Yuki chieftains, because of the Buddha, and of the setting free of the white people? Yea, and a little check in the field shall bring it to a head. Therefore suffer me to remain at my lord's side."

I shook my head. "It has been said, O Halkh," I answered in the Yuki fashion.

He withdrew with an obeisance. Then, looking toward Tamsa, I saw him glowering at me in deep resentment at the rebuke which I had given him.

His face was hot; I think he would have broken into impetuous speech. But suddenly all eyes were turned toward the hanging carpet, brushing past which the Princess Kara came, not as Alma had come, but attended by her maidens.

"What is this, O sister, that, you come here to the council, leaving me alone in the women's apartments?" she cried, looking on Alma angrily. "Though you be queen in this land under Og, and the betrothed of our gracious lord Ruuf, surely I am not unworthy to listen to the same counsel as you—yea, and perchance to speak," she added, flashing a glance at Tamsa.

His own look answered hers, and it was as a revelation to me. For I knew, as surely as if I had been told, that Tamsa had plotted her intervention in order to sway the counsel of the Yuki lords against me, a plot which Alma's innocent action had forestalled.

And, looking at Halkh, I saw his eyes fixed meaningly upon mine, and for the moment my heart misgave me that I had not yielded to his petition. Pride held me from changing; but the clear future seemed suddenly clouded with distrust.

CHAPTER XII

THE PROPHECY

SOMETIMES, IN RARE intervals, I had wondered whether my acts had been in conformity with the wishes of old Malachi. I had seen nothing of the old man, and in my rare encounters with Alma I had had no opportunity to speak of him, nor had I, indeed, thought of him.

I had gathered that Malachi was at the court of Og much as Elijah among the enemy priests of Baal at the court of Ahab. Credited with magical powers it will be remembered that Timour had ascribed his defeat at my hands to these he was part prophet and part captive, part slave and part a guest of honor; but Og and the Yuki feared him. He held the office of Keeper of the Pit-Slaves, now abolished, and in this capacity he had admitted me from the pit into the streets of Nork.

Malachi had given me no instructions, but he had held out a choice; and his prophecies of my success had been ambiguous and even disquieting.

I had meant to speak of him that night to Alma at the banquet, as, seated on golden thrones placed at the foot of Og's in the audience-hall, we leaned toward each other across the body of the king's mare, who crouched before his seat, her bright eyes following every movement of her master's. Yet, with a more momentous question upon my lips, again I forgot.

In Nork, which was ablaze with lights, the Yuki were holding high festival. Inside the palace swarming crowds filled the great court, drinking from great vats of rice-wine, and feasting upon the carcasses of beeves, cooked over bonfires.

Only the watchful archers at their posts in the keep guarded Nork against an irruption of Timour's men. But Halkh was with them, and I felt confident that there would be no surprise. Meanwhile Khom was gathering his ships into port in preparation for the work of the night to come.

In Og's audience-hall the long tables groaned under their viands. The Yuki feasted around us. The festivities were to last almost till daylight, when Alma and I were to be betrothed in accordance with the Yuki ceremonial.

Og, who had been drinking deep out of his horrid goblet, and growing more and more uproarious, was hiccuping out wise aphorisms, which Epsilon was writing down, and would, I suspected, afterward destroy. I leaned toward Alma across the body of the mare.

"Alma," I whispered, "you know of my love for you; and yet I have never heard from your lips whether you love me as women love, or after the fashion of statecraft."

"Surely my lord jests with me," she answered, turning her face away. "How should his favor have fallen upon me, who am unknown to him? Surely it was but a pretense, that day within the Buddha's jaws?"

"Why, Alma?" I asked in astonishment.

"How should my lord, who is acknowledged heir to our empire, have stolen into Nork furtively, and been endangered at Epsilon's hands, unless it was a trick to test me?"

Her lip quivered. She looked across the room, and I followed her glance along the wall to Kara, reclining in her marble chair at the opposite end, attended by two of her women, and surrounded by many of the Yuki nobles.

As I looked upon her, Kara, attracted by my gaze, turned her head and looked back at me calmly, though her fingers played with agitation in the folds of her silken robes.

She seemed to me like a splendid tigress, lying back there

indolently, and planning, I suspected, mischief against us. And yet only a woman of rare courage could have endured the humiliation that she had suffered, and still have shown her face among the courtiers.

"It was no trick, Alma," I answered. "Nor was it necessary to know you in order that I should love you. It was only needful that I should set eyes on you. Tell me you love me, for there is no time for play of words, since to-morrow I leave to battle with Timour for your empire."

She looked straight into my eyes, and, though her voice trembled slightly, her words were simple and frank.

"Yes, I have loved you, too, since I set eyes on you," she answered. "And thereby I knew you to be verily him whom Malachi claimed you to be. For this has been prophesied, that love shall fall between the deliverer and the princess of the captive people, love hard, and bitter, and unfulfilled. And yet, in the end, all shall be well, though not as love had hoped. I know no more than that, my lord, but I love you as a woman loves the man fated from eternity to be hers.

"And therefore my love, and yours, have made me afraid," she continued. "For old Malachi has warned me that I could choose either love for myself or freedom for my people, but not the two. Thus has he warned me from my childhood. And therefore my choice is bitter: for either you shall deliver us, and my love is vain, or, gaining each other, we leave my people enslaved. Yea, enslaved," she whispered in agitation, "for well I know that King Og's proclamation will be withdrawn, either by him or by another."

"I place no faith in Malachi," I answered, more lightly than I felt. "The old man is in his dotage."

For, though the fulfillment of my pledge still hounded me, the sequence of events seemed to have removed it to a long distant time.

"Even though this be so, my lord," she answered, "my heart

is heavy under my double burden. Listen, while I recount briefly to you, for you seem as one whose past is half forgotten.

"This land, the wise men tell us, was once inhabited only by men of our own color. They became luxurious, and fell before the inroads of the Yuki from the cold north whence they had withdrawn when they became too effeminate to hold the iron soil in fee. Westward from Nork extends a whole great continent, and beyond that, they tell us, lies another sea. And there are lands again beyond both oceans. And all these lands were once populous and in our keeping.

"Ages ago the Yuki from the frozen north overran the earth, apportioning each tribe to itself an undefended city for spoil. Nevertheless, in our earth refuges we have looked forward to our deliverance; and the house of Tamsa has ever ruled, even in captivity, because of the brave deeds performed by the first Tamsa against the oppressor.

"King Og, who captured me and my half-sister, Kara, in our infancy, reared us in his palace. He showered gifts upon us, but he oppressed my people. Therefore I plotted to dethrone him, and Tamsa, my kinsman, whom Og had sought to attach also to his cause by gifts, was to have led an army against him, with weapons forged secretly in the depths.

"In spite of the pledge that bound me, this turn of events has changed our plans and linked us all together to uphold Og—at least, until Timour is overthrown.

"But I fear Tamsa, for I know the restless ambition that will never halt until it has secured for him the throne. Aye, my lord, he has long sought me, planning to gain the kingdom with me, and I fear him. Never did he accept you gladly, but saw in you only an obstacle to his own schemes. How long will his faith last, when fortune changes, either for good or ill?

"Yea, O my lord, my heart is deeply troubled with all these things, and because of the enmity of Kara, who never cared that our people were oppressed, as I did. In childhood we loved each

other, and now there seems none loyal to me, save thee and
Halkh."

Her sobbing words contrasted wildly with the merriment
about us, and Og's great rumble.

"There is one thing more that I must say, my lord," continued
Alma. "You heard Timour speak of the vial, whose breaking is
believed to portend the end of the Yuki Empire. It has been
handed down among the princesses of my people from immemorial time, to guard it as their honor.

"Timour has learned something of its properties from traitors among our wise men; but he has not learned all that I know,
and neither I nor our wise men know much beyond what tradition tells us.

"The drinking of a portion of its contents is said by some to
confer immortality. Others say that the princess of the captive
people who shall partake of this in her dire extremity will be
enabled thereby to translate herself bodily into another land,
there to await a change in fortune. Still others say that he who
filled the vial, ages ago, will some day come to claim it, and with
it the princess of that day.

"But all are agreed that, when the last princess's fortunes are
at their lowest ebb, she may, by drinking of this, in some strange
way escape her destiny.

"Take this, and guard it, as you would guard Alma's life, in
proof of my faith," she said, "And part with it in no extremity.
And, at the last, if Timour wins, you and I shall drink of it
together. For my love is deathless, O my Lord Ruuf!"

She stretched out her hand quickly, and I felt something pass
from it into mine, in the shadow of Og's throne.

I looked quickly, to discover that I was holding a little bottle.
What its original composition had been it was impossible to
determine, for it was thickly incrusted with mineral matter,
evidently the accumulation of centuries, and seemed as solid as
stone. I placed it in my girdle, and then, turning by instinct that
I was being watched, I saw Kara's eyes fixed on me once more.

I saw the princess rise, and come, like a lithe panther, down the hall.

She stopped before us and made a profound obeisance. "Hail, my lord! Greetings, O royal sister!" she said softly.

And she dropped upon one knee before Alma.

"Deign to forgive me, sister," she said, "that in my jealousy of thee I permitted my tongue to speak evil words that did not come from my heart. For in truth I wish thee only good. Lo, I am thy loyal servant, and my lord's also!"

Alma leaned forward, and I saw compassionate tears in her eyes.

"Rise, my sister!" she said. "Kneel not to me, for ever since we were children all I have had was thine, and my love also, in as full measure as thou didst ask."

Kara turned toward me. "And my lord," she asked, "will he, too, deign to forgive?"

"I forgive thee, Kara," I answered, "for the past is past, and it need never be remembered."

Kara rose to her feet, and, with another obeisance to both of us, returned to her place amid the group of nobles, who had watched the scene in lively astonishment. What had prompted Kara to this act of humiliation, I wondered? Was she to be trusted? Or did she mask, by her humbleness, some unfathomable scheme?

"My lord, I am happy indeed," said Alma at my side, in answer to my unspoken question. "Kara, jealous though she has always been of me, is loyal at heart. I believe her—do you, too, my Lord Ruuf?"

And I believed, and stilled my doubts, for Alma's sake.

Higher rose the revelry. In the center of the hall, between two lines of tables, a mock contest was taking place. Two Yuki, seated on horseback, with their arms locked about each other, were wrestling. The applause grew wilder. A troupe of dancing girls, who entered, approached the throne, grimacing and posturing, and began a swaying, rhythmical dance. The wrestlers continued their efforts. The courtiers, forming into groups, covered the floor of the audience-hall.

Through it all an increasing uneasiness beset me. Although my past existed as hardly more than a vague instinct in my mind, I hated the scenes about me, and, looking at Alma's gentle face, resolved that if ever the time came when I was ruler in the land, I would restore—

What? I was searching my memory for the scenes I had known before, but could not picture. I left my throne and strolled about the hall, watching the wrestlers, mingling with the courtiers. Presently I found Halkh standing beside me.

He plucked at my sleeve and drew me away.

"There is need of watchfulness, in truth, my lord," he said, "for, when the lion grows old, each jackal has already chosen the tid bit for his feast."

"What do you mean, O Halkh?" I asked, impressed by his earnestness.

"My lord perceived the look on Tamsa's face yesterday?" he asked. "Will he not, then, reconsider his plan, and permit me to attend him in battle?"

"No, O Halkh," I answered. "Thou knowest that thy duty lies at the keep, to guard the two princesses, and Nork, against an irruption of Timour's men. I have spoken; there remains no more to say."

"Yet know that Halkh ever serves his lord in life," he answered, and turned away.

My heart misgave me. Had I been wise, I wondered, in rejecting Halkh's plea? The safety of the keep had appeared paramount; yet perplexity beset me in the midst of my increasing fears, when I had almost yielded to the instinct which bade me change my mind, Og's great voice, booming from his throne, stilled the uproar.

"Harken, O men of the Yuki race!" he cried. "The night is far gone, and to-morrow my son, Ruuf, leads out my troops against Timour. Therefore it is meet that his betrothal to the Princess

Alma be solemnized, in order that the thought of the bride who shall await him may spur him on to victory. But first let my soothsayers prophesy good fortune for my kingdom, and for my son Ruuf and his bride. Speak, Epsilon," he continued, "if, indeed, my own wisdom has not obscured thine own, as the sun obscures the stars."

Epsilon strutted forward in front of the throne, accompanied by his band of priests in yellow.

"Many wise words hast thou deigned to utter this night, great King of the Yuki," he replied. "Yet my powers fail me not, and my eyes are opened, so that the future lies like a written page before me.

"I see thee victor over Timour, thine enemy, and drinking wine from his skull, rimmed with rich gold. And, as for Prince Ruuf and his bride, great honors shall be theirs. Under the shadow of thy might and wisdom they shall live long together, beloved by all who feed upon the honey of thy bounty, king.

"And yet I see these gifts snatched away by one whose anger thou hast kindled, O king. For surely Buddha grants not gifts such as these to those who feed him not, so that his belly is empty, and his spirit faint. Restore the sacrifice, O king, feed the Buddha, who has ever watched over thee and thine, that his wrath may be appeased, and that he may pour his honey over thee!"

At this bold challenge a murmur of approval swelled through the court. Epsilon's demand had manifestly a backing that was considerably greater than mine. Og frowned, bit his lip, and forced himself to a suave answer.

"Truly, O Epsilon, this matter shall be considered," he said, "after the victory. But let it not be said that Og, who feared no man, feared the bronze Buddha. Let the wise man Malachi be searched for and brought to me, in order that I may also hear what his god hath revealed to him."

Suddenly, as if a shadow had come before me, I saw the black-robed figure of Malachi in front of the throne. How he had entered the hall unperceived I do not know; but his sudden appearance there among the feasters seemed to strike the air with a deadly chill.

Og leaned from his throne and stretched out his great hand toward him.

"Greetings, O wise prophet of the white people!" he said ironically. "Thou hast heard the doubtful words of Epsilon: deign, then, to prophesy good fortune to me and to my realm, for verily thou hast much secret wisdom, and never yet hast thou agreed with Epsilon about anything. And since thy prophecies have ever been of evil, old vulture, prophesy good now, inasmuch as Epsilon hath seen no favorable sign."

Old Malachi extended his skinny arms toward the throne.

"Yea. I will prophesy, but not as thou hast bidden me, O king," he answered. "To me, too, hath the future been made clear, O king, thy days are numbered, thy kingdom ended, and even now the hand of death is stretched forth over thee. Thy realm passeth, O king, and in the days that come it shall be but as the memory of a dream."

He turned with a fierce gesture upon Alma and me.

"And as for these," he cried, "who sought their own ends rather than the task laid upon them, verily, I say, they shall desire, but they shall never achieve, and they shall find their joy become ashes, and their hope turn to despair, because of this."

And he was gone, stalking among the silent courtiers like some Daniel of old, and none dared utter a word.

CHAPTER XIII

SUSPICIONS

"**EVER HAS THAT** ill-omened vulture prophesied ill of me and mine," growled Og from his throne. "And, since he prophesies thus, a thought has come to me. Lo, to-morrow night I myself shall lead out my hosts against Timour. And, if it be that Malachi's words are brought to nought, it is in my mind to give him to the bronze Buddha."

Instantly the Yuki nobles clustered about their king, cheering him wildly. The news spread with electrical speed throughout the palace, and the audience-hall was packed.

"Now let old Epsilon, my soothsayer, proclaim the forthcoming marriage of my son Ruuf and the Princess Alma beside him," announced the king.

Old Epsilon stepped forward. "O great king, on such occasions it is customary to propitiate the Buddha with sacrifices," he said. "Therefore let my lord make an exception to his rule and feed old Malachi to him, that we may see which is stronger, Malachi or the Buddha."

Tumultuous cheering greeted this announcement. Og stirred uneasily upon his throne, looking at me.

"If it please my lord, there shall be no sacrifices for us," I said.

"So I have said," grumbled the king. "Therefore proceed with the ceremony, O Epsilon."

Old Epsilon complied, scowling. The assembly ringed us round, gathering about the grille before the Buddha's jaws in the passage behind the throne. And, recalling my last adventure there, I shuddered with a very lively fear.

What if old Epsilon, by some trick, should contrive to send me through the grille against the grinding teeth?

However, nothing of the sort happened. The hand of yellow-robed priests intoned some litany, to the music of the assembled fife-players. And, behold, Alma and I were looking into each other's eyes, happy and unashamed, with all the felicity of a common life before us.

Yet even then my fears increased; it seemed to me that this cup of happiness, so near my lips, might yet be dashed down. The ceremony in itself had no binding effect; it corresponded to the old betrothal.

And somehow there welled up into my mind memories of another life and land, where no grim-visaged Buddha looked down on betrothed couples, and I longed with all my heart to be with Alma somewhere where no whisper of the court could ever come to us.

I accompanied her with her women to the women's apartments. There, while her maids kept a discreet distance, we exchanged a few hasty words.

"I shall return victorious over Timour, O my princess," I said. "And all our troubles shall be swept away."

And I rallied her upon her anxious looks.

"In truth, how can I but be troubled, my Lord Ruuf," she said, "with the words of old Malachi in my ears, and thee departing, and not knowing if thou or Timour will be the conqueror? Let my lord grant me a boon!"

"It is granted before it is uttered," I answered.

But she changed her mind and would not ask it. At last I had to go. I could not resist kissing her, in spite of the presence of her decorous handmaid, Mnerma, who looked inexpressibly shocked at this salutation, unknown among the Yuki. So we parted.

But I lingered in the palace, like any boy beneath the window of his love, picturing the days that were to come, and girding myself with courage for the battle with Timour.

I looked down into the illuminated streets, and heard the multitudes below shouting my name and Alma's. And yet a sense of inexpressible loneliness was upon me, and but for Alma I hardly know how I could have endured my life.

At last I turned to go, when suddenly, in the half-darkened corridor, I saw a female figure, which seemed to have come from the direction of the women's apartments, flitting before me.

As I watched it I saw it go toward the audience-hall, in which King Og still sat, drinking with a few of his favorite retainers.

Bewildered at this, I followed. Suddenly the figure turned and seemed to disappear into the wall before my eyes.

I followed more quickly, and all at once I realized that she had passed through the secret entrance by which Alma had led me back into the palace corridor out of the Buddha's belly. So hasty had been her flight that she had not stopped to secure the door behind her.

I glanced hurriedly about me. No one was stirring, and the black pages had gathered at the far end of the corridor to watch the illuminations in the streets below. Hastily I stepped through the entrance.

I was in complete darkness, but I heard the rustle of the woman's dress beneath me, and I remembered the many flights of stairs that led downward into the maze of tunnels beneath the palace.

I descended after her. Though my sandals clacked on the stone stairs, she did not cry out or seem to notice my presence behind her. At first I thought that she was one of the deaf and blind fife-players.

But suddenly I heard her stop; then I heard her breathing at my side. She placed her arms about my neck.

"I have come to thee, O Hagris, to keep my promise," she

said. "But for a moment only, to assure thee of my love for thee, as I told thee."

She drew her hand across my face, and suddenly screamed. It was plain that she had mistaken me for another, that I had stumbled upon a love-tryst.

Still crying out in a shrill voice, she turned and ran down the stairs. I thought that she was going to the belly of the Buddha, but suddenly I heard a door grate on its hinges, and, reaching out, I managed to catch it before the catch snapped behind the fleeing woman.

Perhaps it was indecorous to pursue her further, but I was prompted by more than curiosity. I felt that her presence there portended no good to Alma; and there was something ironical in this pursuit of the decorous Mnerma, who had looked so shocked at my parting embrace with Alma.

As I opened the door a little light shone in from a lamp of reeds, bound together and steeped in oil, that hung on the stone wall of a wide tunnel.

Mnerma stopped and glanced backward. I remained hidden in the recesses out of the illumination of the lamp, and, apparently thinking that I had been shaken off the scent, she went forward more slowly. Then, out of the darkness at the other end of the tunnel, I saw a Yuki soldier advance to greet her.

I did not hesitate to watch them, for their meeting was of the austere and formal nature characteristic of Yuki lovers. It was a brief one, too. After the lapse of a few minutes the soldier turned and disappeared, and Mnerma came tripping back, and passed through the entrance, closing the door behind her and never noticing me.

The catch was, of course, upon the inner side. It was easy for me to return. But I was more curious than ever about the meeting—not as regarded Alma, for the fears I had entertained had vanished in the light of the commonplace discovery of its cause; but as to the manner in which the soldier had gained access to the tunnel.

I did not know where it ran. Certainly it did not run toward the belly of the Buddha. Was there another entrance to the pit of the slaves?

I followed behind the soldier, hearing his feet before me upon the flags with which the tunnel was paved. Presently I became conscious of a pressure upon my ear-drums.

Then I knew where I was. My foster-father had often told me of the tunnels built under the rivers by the prehistoric race that founded Nork. It was evidently one of these.

The pressure, which had increased, gradually decreased, however. I began to hear the lapping of water in the distance. Then to my amazement, I saw a star, low in the sky, before me. And I stopped as I saw the soldier at the water's-edge.

The floor of the tunnel was level with the surface of the river. And I remembered how it was that in former days the river ran at a much higher level, so that the tunnel, which had formerly been under water, now projected, like a huge pipe, for a short distance above the surface to the point where it had broken. The pressure upon my ears was caused by the higher level of the dammed river at the royal docks.

I found a recess in the tunnel's wall, and, hiding myself in it, I watched the soldier step into a boat that was waiting. But he did not pull out into the river. He rested there as if waiting for some one to arrive.

Then the tramp of footsteps rang along the tunnel floor, and I thanked the impulse that had prompted me to conceal myself where I was. For, swinging past me, so close that his yellow robes almost brushed mine, came Epsilon, and with him two priests, and two of Og's guards, swords by their sides, and on their faces the evident intention of using them at the least pretext.

And after them came a man whose face I could not see, for he wore a short, semi-transparent black veil, after the fashion of the country Yuki. Long the group stood beside the boat, conversing eagerly, but in such low tones that no word of what was said came to my ears.

Only, somehow, the idea grew on me that this veiled man was Tamsa. In vain I tried to banish it. He was of Tamsa's build, he had his gestures, and his presence there with Epsilon, if he was Tamsa, boded ill to the success of our enterprise. For I knew that Epsilon would stoop at nothing to defeat me, if not his royal master.

After what must have been the better part of an hour Epsilon and one of the guards entered the boat. The soldier pulled down-stream with oars that made only the faintest ripple in the water. He passed the black hulks of Khom's vessels, riding at their anchorage, and seemed to direct his course toward the opposite shore.

There was a good deal of contraband trade between the two coasts, which was winked at by the watching navies, but there was no place for such contraband as Epsilon.

Very thoughtfully I returned, making fast the doors behind me, and at length I found myself in my own quarters in the palace.

CHAPTER XIV

THE CROSSING

ON THE NEXT day Epsilon was missing from the palace precincts.

I kept my counsel. No one suspected that he had gone over to Timour, and in the preparations for our departure there was little speculation about his absence. Khom could not move his ships, which were marshaled along the shore, till after nightfall, but there was an endless amount of work to be done.

First there was the quiet marshaling of our forces, in small companies, just outside the walls of the city, where it could foregather hidden from the sight of Timour's lookouts upon the hills on the opposite shore, being concealed behind the high ruins along the lower shores of the island.

There was the provisioning of the ships that were to carry us and our supplies, and this, too, had to be done cautiously, lest any inkling of our purpose should reach Timour.

There was the completion of the temporary piers that had been erected at the embarkation point above the rapids.

The populace, among whom the rumor of our intentions had spread, had been forbidden to cheer; but they were assembled in the streets to greet us, so thickly that it was with difficulty we could clear a passage. And when the giant form of Og, borne in his litter by eight bearers—since there was no horse that could carry him—appeared upon the street, all the commands were forgotten, and Yuki and whites alike went wild with joy. They pressed about him, cheering ecstatically.

For all knew that the victory of Timour meant the restoration of the old order of things; and there was no man there who had not felt the gall of the Yuki yoke.

The palace, which covered the lower portion of the island, and was in itself a little city, was accessible from two sides only. One fronted the river, and was guarded by Halkh, with his archers, by means of the keep that commanded the bridge. The other was northward, through the gateway leading into the great court. But the great bronze gates which guarded this were invulnerable against anything but the heaviest battering-rams, and these could not be brought up by surprise; consequently, a guard of a dozen archers was all that was needed here.

I bade Halkh farewell. He did not repeat his warnings, but held my hands in his own and raised them to his lips.

"Let my lord remember the vow of his servant, Halkh, to be his true henchman in life and death," he said. "For, even as I serve the Princess Alma, so I serve thee."

I left him and rode out to join my men. The great bronze gates closed behind us, not to be opened again till our victorious return. Without delaying at the temporary camping-ground, where the bulk of our forces were waiting to take up the march, we moved on our way northward.

It was an eery sensation, riding out in the darkness with that great host about me. I could only see the nearer files; but there was the indescribable feel of the multitudes behind, and I knew that upon me devolved the leadership of all these, for Og, in his litter, was drinking again, though he had finished his last bout but an hour before.

His presence served as an encouragement to the Yuki soldiers, among whom the tradition of his former prowess had become a tradition; but his day was past, and he would be no vital figure in the campaign—if anything, an embarrassment.

The light cavalry of the clansmen had been sent on ahead an hour before. In the van marched those of Halkh's bowmen who had not been left on guard at the gates. They were all picked men, and an important factor—more than their number might have appeared to warrant, for Timour had none who could compete with them.

After them came our eight hundred heavily armored men, in companies led by their clan chiefs, with myself at their head on horseback; and behind these came Og, rolling in his litter, carried by the panting bearers. Tamsa, with his white regiment, brought up the rear.

For some miles we pursued our march in complete silence, until at length the line halted, and the word was whispered back that Khom's ships had made the passage of the rapids safely, and were lying in wait for us off shore.

The embarkation was not a difficult process, but it was complicated by an unforeseen incident which was destined to have a considerable effect upon our fortunes.

For Og's eight bearers, carrying his litter up the wet gangway, found the task beyond their powers, and, as they stopped, one of them slipped and fell, bringing down the litter with a crash like a falling block.

The great king rolled on the slippery gangway, and it took all the efforts of his bearers to prop him back from the edge. He rose to his feet, bellowing like a wild steer.

"By the great Buddha, I go no further!" he roared. "It is an unfavorable omen. Where is my chief soothsayer?"

"My lord, he has not accompanied us," said one of the king's attendants.

"Doth Epsilon remain behind in the palace, to bring misfortunes upon our enterprise?" roared Og. "Ruuf, my son, take the command, for if the adventure is to fail, I had rather misfortune came upon thee than upon me."

And he stretched himself in his litter again, and the bearers, who had counted on a respite, began puffing back toward Nork, attended by Og's body-guard of twenty men.

This delayed us, but we embarked quickly, and the ships, pushing in as close as possible to the shallows of the Baruk-

Halin shore, dropped anchor there, and man and horse swam across the intervening reach of the stream.

We quickly marshaled our forces on the opposite bank. The first part of our task was accomplished safely, and it was clear that Timour had no scouts posted in the vicinity.

I had listened for the distant sounds of the feigned attack by the bridge, but had heard nothing, nor had any of us. This rather troubled me; however, the wind was blowing from the north, and it was quite possible that the sounds would not have reached us at that distance.

We passed forward, carrying on our saddle supplies for two or three days, leaving the remainder to be brought up by the seamen. There was a range of low hills about seven miles inland. Here I had decided to encamp at dawn, beyond the Yellow River. The position would place us well upon Timour's flank, and a reconnaissance in the morning would determine whether it was advisable to press forward for immediate battle or to fortify and supply our position and enter upon a campaign of a more lengthy nature.

After we had been traveling for some distance Tamsa came riding up from the rearguard and placed his horse alongside of mine.

"Our adventure has fared well thus far, my Lord Ruuf," he began, "and fortunate it is that Og turned back, for there may be unexpected difficulties awaiting us."

"None that we have not already discounted, O Tamsa," I answered. "For, at the worst, Timour has had warning of our approach, and has kept his forces together. Still, we outnumber him. The alternative is not of conquest and defeat, but of an easy and a difficult victory."

"Yea, my lord, words sound fair when they come from the desires of the speaker," he returned. "May the bronze Buddha grant that my lord's aspirations find fulfillment!"

And he fell back, leaving me to wonder at his meaning, and why he had ridden up to announce his fears. However, I let the matter slip from my mind as I rode on. It was a difficult march by the faint light of the stars, over a camel track bestrewn with boulders, and bordered by ruins overgrown with shrubs; while the bifurcations, which were numerous, made it necessary for us to retrace our steps several times.

We were still a good distance from our destination when the unexpected appearance of the quarter-moon on the horizon warned us that dawn was not far away.

I summoned Tamsa and the chiefs of the Yuki clans to a conference.

"How far is it hence to our camping-place?" I asked.

"Let my lord take heart, for it is not far," answered Tamsa. "I recognize this region well, by those hills in the distance, for it was along this road that we went when Og sent me upon his mission to invite Timour to visit him. Yonder lies the Yellow River, and, once past it, the march to the camping-ground is not a long one, if the fords be unguarded."

"The map of Baruk-Halin shows two fords," I said.

"There are two, my lord, and that map was drawn up by my own hand. The first lies half a mile eastward of us, and the second twice as far to the northwest. Of these the nearer is the shorter road, but it is more likely to conceal an ambuscade.

"Do you, my lord, take a man, then, from among your guard, and reconnoiter the further ford," he continued, "while I will take one of mine and test the passage of the nearer?"

I assented, and, selecting one of my men, set out over the broken ground. The journey seemed longer than Tamsa had said, but at length the low brush through which we had been riding gave place to open, shelving ground that ran down toward the stream. Bidding my man wait for me, I rode my horse quickly across the open ground in the direction of the river below.

I halted upon the edge and looked to the right and left. The ford seemed unguarded. I was about to turn my horse when I

felt a smart tap upon the saddle-flap, and, looking down, saw
something sticking into it.

I drew out the broken shaft of an arrow.

Almost at the same instant there came the hiss of a feathered
shaft in flight, passing above me. Had I not stooped to see the
saddle-flap it would probably have pierced my face to the brain.
I swung round, and discerned a bowman crouching among
some ruins at the edge of the brush, not twenty paces away,
holding a relaxed bow in his hand, and peering after his missile.

It was so dark that I saw him only as an indistinct shadow
among the trees, and he would have escaped my notice altogether, but for the unmistakable attitude of the archer.

I wheeled my horse and rode at him at a gallop, at the same
time drawing my sword to cut him down. He hastily fitted a
third arrow to his string and fired. The shaft flew wide, and he
ran back among the bushes. When I reached the place where
he had been I could find no trace of him.

I rode back, to find my follower waiting for me. A glance at
his face showed me that he was ignorant of what had happened.

I galloped back to the halting-place, to find Tamsa already
there. Though his journey had been the shorter, his horse was
breathing heavily, and, touching it with my hand, I found that
its flank was covered with sweat. Tamsa must have ridden hard.

I had decided, during my ride back, that the solitary archer
was merely some robber, such as abounded along the caravan
and camel roads, even so near to Nork. There was no danger;
still, I was about to mention the episode when Tamsa blurted
out:

"My lord, the east ford is clear, and I have awaited your return
to ask that the army take that route, since dawn is approaching,
and we should take up our position before daylight."

I assented, and, at my order, the waiting cavalry went trotting
down to the ford. The footmen followed them; we crossed the
river, waist-deep, and rode up a straggling path into the hills.

Presently the road terminated in an extensive plateau. A

glance showed that this was an ideal camping-ground, for it was protected on the left flank by a high elevation, and commanded a view of the valleys around. Accordingly I ordered the camp to be pitched, and sent a messenger to turn back the cavalry.

As the line halted Tamsa and the Yuki chiefs came riding up to me.

"Surely this is not the appointed camping-place, my Lord Ruuf!" protested Tamsa. "A little further, and we reach the heights from which we can sweep down upon the undefended cities of Baruk-Halin."

"Let us rest here, O Tamsa," I rejoined, "for our men are weary, and would be at a disadvantage in case of a surprise. Let them rest, therefore, and the horses also, except one company, which shall reconnoiter the heights in front of us."

Tamsa uttered an angry exclamation; then, checking himself, departed on the mission I had given him. The Yuki leaders looked at one another with scowls. They uttered no protest, but it was plain that they were not in the mood for delays. Already they had been talking of plunder before the morning passed.

But the tired soldiers, receiving my order with delight, stripped off their armor and accouterments, and began gathering brushwood to build their fires, which, kindled from sparks struck by their bow-drills, soon blazed on the plateau, between the tents.

CHAPTER XV

FACE TO FACE

THE DAWN CAME quickly. The white patch in the sky grew golden, the air grew light, the sun's rim appeared over the hills, and suddenly a flood of golden sunlight illuminated the land, sweeping away the curling mists from the hollows of the hills.

Hardly was the sun up when my men sprang to their feet, pointing excitedly toward the hills. Raising my eyes, I saw bodies of horsemen watching us from every vantage point.

At the same time our scouts came galloping in. They informed us that they had encountered Timour's cavalry, his vanguard, on the heights, and had seen the approach of his main army along the road below, not an hour's journey away. From the length of the dust clouds that concealed it, it was evident that the feint of Halkh and Khom had failed to cause him to divide his forces.

But our situation was good, though this involved a disappointment. We had crossed the river, which could have been held against us, and were prepared to give Timour battle in his own territory, with every prospect of success, so long as our light horse, which numbered about as many as his, were able to hold the ford and prevent his cutting our communications with the ships.

Still, it was fortunate that I had not let myself be persuaded by Tamsa to advance further into the hills, where we should have been surrounded.

I formed my men up on the plateau, which, as I have said,

was admirably adapted to defense, its left side being inaccessible, leaving it vulnerable only upon the right flank and on the front. In the center I placed our eight hundred heavy-armed troops, ranged in their companies according to their clans, with our few archers posted in the intervals among them.

Upon the right, guarding the flank of the plateau, I posted Tamsa's white regiment, light troops not suited to bearing the shock of Timour's heavy-armed legionaries but suitable for defensive work, or for following up an attack. They were ranged in echelon, for mobility, and on the extreme right I placed the light horse in extended squadrons. Their purpose there was either to support Tamsa's light-armed troops, in case the brunt of battle fell on them, or to head off any movement of Timour's cavalry to seize the ford and cut our communications.

Thus my left wing, practically unassailable, was to be the pivot on which my troops could be swung, like the hand of a clock, moving fastest at its tip, the horsemen, in a circular movement which was to cut off Timour's retreat through the passes while my left pinned him down.

It was not long before Timour's army came into sight, debouching along the road through the mountains. It was a splendid sight, that marshaling of his hosts before our eyes, less than a mile across the valley, and one that made my heart beat quickly. With drums throbbing and fifes shrilling, and pennons streaming above the array of gleaming swords, Timour's army advanced and extended upon a long ridge that fronted the plateau.

Then, moving to the right and left as swiftly as flowing water, Timour's horsemen shot out and extended on either wing, to take stock of our defenses, riding up to within fifty paces of the plateau and uttering defiant cries.

Timour did not mean to attack immediately, however. In proof of this he began to encamp, and soon the long lines of black goatskin tents confronted ours across the valley. His own tent was pitched in the center; it was square in form, and a long yellow pennon flew from each of the corners.

As these maneuvers were in progress I saw the Yuki chiefs conferring. Then Khai, the man who had opposed me at the council table, came galloping up to where I rode among the archers, posting them advantageously. After him came the others, pell-mell, brandishing their curved yataghans.

"Now let my lord give the command to advance, and we shall scatter them as the wheat-husks are scattered upon the thresh-ing-floor!" he cried.

Cheers from the swordsmen about me greeted this speech, which Khai delivered at the top of his voice, and they were taken up all along our lines, while presently counter-cries came from Timour's lines.

"What say you, Tchar?" I asked another.

"The same!" he cried. "Let my lord give the word, and, as the vulture swoops on the carrion, so shall we swoop, on Timour."

"And you, O Ngiddo?" I asked one of the older and soberer men.

"I am for delay," he answered. "Does my lord not see that the sun shines into our faces, so that our archers will be at a disad-vantage? Besides, our men have marched all night, while Timour doubtless has rested near at hand. Furthermore," he continued, looking calmly into the angry faces about him, "I would counsel delay until to-morrow, and also that our horsemen be instruct-ed to retire before Timour's, so that he may think we shun the battle. For, if his impetuosity leads him to attack, we fight here at an advantage."

"The wise words of an old man!" said Tamsa, sneering. He had ridden up among the circle of the chiefs and was watching me furtively, but without addressing me.

"Yet, had I followed your earlier counsel, O Tamsa," I re-turned, "we should by now have been entrapped in the hills."

He muttered something in a sulky manner, and Khai, spur-ring his horse up to mine, reined in within a foot of me and gesticulated fiercely with his mailed hand.

"Is it your purpose, then, lord, to remain encamped here, like women sojourning beside the holy waters in prayer for fair sons?" he asked. "Aye, my lord," he flashed out. "I see that with thee there prevail the same prudent counsels as before. Had we assailed Timour's ships boldly, we should by now be riding into his capital."

The other chiefs shouted in approval, and throwing up their bonnets, caught them upon the points of their swords. But I was convinced that Ngiddo's words were wise. They coincided with my own views. I believed that Timour's ardor would lead him to fling himself against the strength of our defenses; for the same demands that were made upon me for instant action were undoubtedly directed against him by his own leaders as well.

Besides, so long as we remained camped in his land he lay under the stigma of cowardice unless he attacked us.

"O Khai, restrain your eagerness," I answered. "For to-morrow is not far away, and then perchance, if Timour has not attacked, our men will be rested and better prepared for the fatigues of the encounter."

Khai turned away angrily. The news of my decision spread swiftly along the lines, and angry looks and mumblings followed me as I rode past.

I felt assured that Timour meant to attack that day, but the hours passed, and still he remained in camp. The only action was among the cavalry. Small encounters were taking place constantly as the two parties tested each other's strength, resolving themselves chiefly into a succession of duels, in which we lost eight men and Timour twelve. Toward the middle of the afternoon Timour, having apparently satisfied himself that his horsemen could not seize the ford, withdrew them.

Then from the ridge there rode out a strange figure. As it drew near it resolved itself into a yellow-robed priest on a brown horse, carrying a long trumpet. It halted some fifty paces from the slope of the plateau, and I recognized old Epsilon.

He set the trumpet to his lips and blew a loud blast. At once every sound on the plateau was hushed, and our men leaned forward, craning their necks to listen.

"O men of Og, and ye white camp-followers, hear the words of Timour, Prince of the Yuki!" cried the old man. "Ye know the cause of this warfare, because King Og, having invited Prince Timour to his court, to wed the Princess Alma, sent him away with shameful insults intolerable to any man of Yuki blood.

"Furthermore, ye know the wrong that has been done to the bronze Buddha, our Lord, who hath ever guarded the Yuki realms, so that his belly goes empty, and his wrath rages over the land. Wherefore it hath been decreed to me that our Lord Buddha hath taken away his empire from the hands of Og, the deluded, and given it to Timour.

"Timour is merciful, and would fain spare those of you who have been led astray by the false words of the impostor, Ruuf, the swineherd's son. Wherefore, men of the Yuki, I counsel you to bind and deliver up this Ruuf to him, and throw yourselves upon great Timour's mercy, that ye may live. For ye know that ye fight for a losing cause, in that the bronze Buddha hath turned his face away from you."

The effect of this speech was instantly apparent. Some of my men, chiefly those who had been personally attached to Og, answered Epsilon with cries of derision; but I saw many of them eying me darkly, and whispering with one another, as if they were only too anxious to comply with Epsilon's invitation.

If the rot of sedition spread, an early attack against Timour would be essential, that it might be stayed.

I moved forward and cried to Epsilon from the edge of the plateau:

"O Epsilon, false priest of a lying god, go back to Timour and give him this message from Ruuf, the son of Og, who speaks to him direct and does not attempt to weaken him by intriguing with his men. Bid him skulk in his tent no longer, since he who overcame him in Og's gardens is prepared to throw him again, if he will dare accept the challenge and lead out his forces to battle. And thus say: 'Dares be, who dared not draw his sword against Og, dare draw it against Og's son?'"

Then I turned around and addressed my own men.

"Moreover," I said, "ye know that the sacrifices which have been made before the Buddha are abhorrent to him, and that because of these he has permitted armed hosts to overrun your land and make captives and slaves of you. What are ye, Yuki men, better than the white race that came before you?"

It was an audacious plea, but I knew the smoldering fires of resentment against Timour, and Og, too, in the hearts of the peasant soldiers, the earlier Yuki branch that had been overthrown. And it succeeded. For ringing shouts went up, and swords were waved, and helmets tossed, and all along the line the cries broke out, until they were caught up by the horsemen and echoed down to the ford.

Old Epsilon waved his arms furiously at me in answer, and, calling down atrocious curses on me, turned his horse and spurred back toward his lines.

It was now late in the afternoon, and it was evident that Timour did not mean to attack that day. I was riding along the lines, pondering whether or not to attack him on the morrow, when Tamsa came galloping toward me, reined in, and rode by my side.

"Will my lord hear me?" he inquired with a sour smile. "I do not come to urge my lord to battle, since I have spoken what is in my heart."

"I will hear you, O Tamsa," I made answer.

"It was last night, upon the march, that I spoke of difficulties that lay before us," Tamsa continued. "Perchance this day's events have inclined my lord to lend his ear more willingly. For the difficulties which I had in mind lay in our own ranks, and not in the arts of the enemy. My lord knoweth that there still remains among my whites much feeling against their Yuki allies."

"It will pass with victory, O Tamsa."

"Yet there exists that which may again kindle those ancient hates," he retorted. "Dare I speak plainly unto my lord, as if we were fellow and fellow, instead of lord and servant?"

"Speak what is in your heart, O Tamsa, for better frankness of speech than a rankling grievance."

"I speak then of the Princess Alma, O my lord Ruuf," said Tamsa. "My lord knows how, at the time of his coming, the white people were preparing to rise and cast off the yoke of Og, and restore her kingdom unto her."

"Aye, Tamsa!"

"For this reason they looked to my Lord Ruuf to lead them, being further deluded by the false words of Malachi, who proclaimed that my lord was not of such flesh and blood as theirs, but had been raised up from the dead for them. Yea, I, too, was among those deluded ones for a space, but afterward I saw that this lie of Malachi's was but to delude the people and make them docile. For that I hold nothing against him, for the common people must ever be deceived. Yet now they mumble, saying that Ruuf has become the servant of Og, and that their hopes are shattered."

"I see no cause for mumbling, O Tamsa, since already they have won their freedom, and without bloodshed."

"My lord speaks truly. But my lord is pledged to the princess. And my lord has heard the old tradition of the vial, handed down among the princesses of the captivity. Is my lord aware of its purpose?"

"I have heard what was said by Timour in the presence of Og."

"Yea, but my lord is half of Yuki blood," said Tamsa. "Now he is Yuki, and now white, as the occasion serves, as if a man should blow on a spoon of broth to make it cool, and, with the same breath, to heat it."

"Speak plainly, O Tamsa."

"Yea, lord, for now I put the pieces of my argument together. The purpose of this vial, which contains nothing but a deadly poison, is to preserve the princesses of the captivity against contaminating the blood of the royal line by mating with any of Yuki blood.

"Therefore, O my lord, if it will please thee to relinquish the Princess Alma on this account, thou canst, as the son of Og, command the faith and loyalty of the white race of Nork, and canst have anything that thou wilt. But otherwise I am inclined to think that my people will follow thee only halfheartedly."

It was impossible for Tamsa to disguise the vehemence of his plea behind the smoothness of the words; and the cool insolence of his demand stung me to the quick.

"O Tamsa, I have heard thee," I replied.

"My lord have mercy on his servant," muttered Tamsa, in the conventional Yuki formula.

"But there is this more to be said. I do not seek counsel upon such matters; yet, since thou hast spoken of my Yuki blood, know that, by virtue of this same blood, Ruuf, the son of Og, has ears that hear for long distances."

"If any enemy has spoken ill of me—" began Tamsa hotly.

"Equally by land and water, O Tamsa, and in the tunnels beneath the Palace of Og, my father."

He started and recovered himself; the movement had been almost imperceptible, but I had been watching for it, and I was sure now that the veiled man in the tunnel had been Tamsa, and that he had been there to play a game of his own.

"Will not my lord speak plainly, in his turn?" he asked.

"Nay, Tamsa, for when obscure speech conveys the meaning clearly, plain speech is discourteous," I answered, dismissing him with a wave of my hand.

CHAPTER XVI

TREASON

WE HAD REACHED the end of the plateau. Before me extended a flat arm of the valley between our hosts, reaching for about a mile and a half to the ford. Along this my cavalry patrols were placed at intervals. I rode slowly toward them, with the purpose of warning them to be on the alert against raids during the night.

Tamsa waited till I had ridden some distance and then went back in the direction of his own regiment, to plot I knew not what mischief there. I was troubled over our interview. It threw his hostility toward me into a clear focus.

His looks had shown his discomfiture; but had I been wise in disclosing my hand to him? Would it not precipitate any evil intentions that he might be forming against me?

The purpose of his communication had been unmistakable. He had, in plain words, offered me his allegiance if I would give up the Princess Alma. But to relinquish her, assuming such a thing conceivable, meant to relinquish the throne to her husband, who, I doubted not, was, in Tamsa's own mind, Tamsa. What, then, had Tamsa offered me?

Accustomed from childhood to the oblique speech of the ceremonial code, which was common even among the peasantry, I could interpret Tamsa's meaning. If I would hand over the leadership to him, with Alma, he would secure for me the throne of Timour.

Less guarded than he, I had been drawn into a threat. I had

let him know that his intrigues were not secret from me, while I had the disadvantage of not knowing their extent, nor whether they actually involved him with Timour.

For the first time I recalled the incident beside the ford—the lurking bowman, and then Tamsa's hard-ridden horse—and wondered whether Tamsa had stooped to plan my death.

But I would not let myself believe this. I was riding slowly toward my horsemen when, looking over the ford, along the road which we had traversed, far in the distance I saw two riders galloping toward the camp.

I put my horse to the trot, resolved to meet them, for none but messengers from Nork would be traversing that road at such a time as this. I passed the cavalry patrols, but did not call to any to accompany me, and, since the ridge of the crest concealed the riders from their view, they did not know the purpose of my ride.

I crossed the river, and, topping the ridge behind, perceived the riders, still a long distance away, and then three other horsemen, evidently in pursuit of them, galloping across a transverse road with the clear intention of cutting them off before they reached the river.

I spurred my mount, which, fresh after the day of inactivity, responded to my urging as if he understood. There was perhaps a mile and a half to cover—the two riders were separated from their pursuers by as much, but the course of each party inevitably brought them nearer together.

The fugitives were urging their horses to the utmost, but these were obviously weary, and their response was growing less. I read that in the short, choppy stride of the weary animals.

The three pursuers were Yuki scouts. They galloped at a furious pace, uttering loud yells and waving their yataghans. The parties met.

I saw one of the fugitives lunge at a Yuki, to be instantly cut down. He fell dead from his saddle, and the riderless horse, turning, galloped back along the road by which it had come.

Then my heart leaped in my throat, for I saw that the second fugitive was a woman.

More—it was Alma! I saw her face clear in the rays of the declining sun, and, as the Yuki seized her, I galloped up to them.

One held the girl upon her horse, but without violence; the two others rode at me with flashing yataghans. There was a moment of cut and parry, then my sword lunged home in the breast of the nearer swordsman.

The weapon of the second fell slanting-wise upon my helm, which I had fortunately put on, denting it and sending me reeling in the saddle; but before he could recover his weapon I had withdrawn my sword from the body of his companion and slashed him through the neck.

The man uttered a scream and galloped away, clinging about his horse's mane, while the blood streamed from the wound. The man who held Alma hesitated an instant, and then, seeing my horsemen who had been attracted by the shouting, topping the ridge behind me, fled for safety, leaving Alma clinging to her saddle and swaying weakly toward me.

She fell into my arms with a little cry of joy. I held her upon her horse and led it back toward our lines, surrounded by our wondering troops, who clustered eagerly about us, whispering to one another.

As for Tamsa, when he saw me return with Alma, his face grew darker than ever. The Yuki chiefs, too, eyed us strangely. I fancied that they believed the girl had come at my demand, for some purpose connected with a bargain with Timour.

But I had no time to disillusion them then. I placed the girl in one of the tents, and set a guard about it, ordering him to admit no one. She was conscious and unharmed, but weak from the long ride, and though she signified that she wished to speak to me at once, I thought it better that she should rest and eat first.

She acquiesced in my decision, but her eagerness was so pitiful that, after about the half of an hour, I made my way back to her. I was surprised to see that the sentry had gone, and as I strode up Tamsa emerged. His face was convulsed with anger, and he did not see me, for as I approached he turned to speak to Alma, standing half within the entrance.

He spoke in a low tone, vibrant with passion, but I could hear nothing of the words. And, as I drew nearer, he turned abruptly and made his way out across the plateau toward his regiment, striding past me and not knowing me.

I went in. Already I had begun to fear that Alma's journey had some reason more intimately connected with ourselves than with the announcement of Khom's failure. That in itself would not have justified the risk she had run in making that wild ride into Baruk-Halin. I saw her standing in the middle of the tent, with her hands clenched and her face white.

She started when she saw me, ran toward me, and burst into tears. In a moment our arms were about each other, and for the first time in our lives we were together with a moment's leisure and none to see. And in her embrace my hopes, my confidence, came back.

"Ruuf, my lord, forgive me for my unqueenly weakness," she said, trying to smile. "But we are surrounded by enemies, and you and Halkh alone seem faithful. Often I have seemed to wander in a wild dream, so disloyal are they who have pledged their faith to me. Kara has gone over to Timour, taking with her a multitude of the white people whom her emissaries have taught that I have betrayed them."

"Kara! From Nork?" I cried.

She nodded.

"Our cause has gone from bad to worse," she said. "Og feasts with the few followers who are left to him, ignorant that, one by one, his leaders are slipping away, and there is none who dares to tell him of it. Thus Epsilon has gone, and all know that he is a weather-vane to catch the shifting wind.

"My lord, when you bade me farewell so short a time ago, but so long to me, it was in my heart to follow you. I even framed a plea to be allowed to accompany you, but refrained, fearing your displeasure. Do not think harshly of me, my lord, for, though love bade me, it was duty brought me.

"You had not left Nork six hours when Mnerma, my hand-maid, made a confession to me upon her knees, asking pardon of me that she had hidden what she had learned.

"She has a lover who is one of Timour's men, and came to Og's court with him, afterward remaining in Nork for the purpose of espionage.

"From him she gathered that a plot is afoot in Nork, whereby if Timour wins the city is to be yielded to him, and Og put to death by those who are now feasting and drinking with him, and deluding his failing mind with tales of victory.

"She feared to come to me, but at last summoned up her courage to do so. I went to Kara's room, planning to question her. I believed her loyal, but I thought that she could help me—she who was once a sister to me. I knew her power among the few of the Yuki leaders who remained with us. But she was gone—to Timour, her frightened maidens faltered; for, insolent in her security, she had told them so.

"I came to you, my lord, to warn you of this, and lo, even in your camp I find disloyalty!"

"Tamsa!" I cried impulsively, and repented my word as soon as I had uttered it, seeing the sad look on Alma's face.

"My lord, I spoke of him," she answered. "Tamsa is my own kinsman, and, ambitious though he is, I will not lose my faith in him. He hates you, but he fights against Timour. Let us hold fast to our faith in him and in all others, Ruuf, until we know them for traitors. How else can we trust any one?"

"Tamsa was in the tent with you, dear Alma," I answered. "He left with the look of a man embittered and desperate. Tell me what passed between you, if no faith be violated thereby, so that I may be armed with this knowledge, and judge him out of it."

"Tamsa has long loved me," answered Alma. "He desires me

and the throne, and, though he claims to desire me the more, I think he deceives himself. Always I have known of these two passions in him. But to-night he was more desperate than I have seen him before; and yet, though his words were evil, I do not believe he would prove false to you.

"He told me that, if I would wed him, he would unite all races under him, and make you chief of Timour's land, or of any of the five kingdoms, traitor though you were. Aye, it was these words that aroused my scorn, my lord. For, when he began to tell me that he had the proofs of this, I drove him from my tent. How could I listen when I love you, Ruuf? No words, but only the disappearance of that vial I gave you, my gift to my future husband, according to our ancient custom—nothing but that could shake my faith, and perhaps not even that."

Her arms were about me still; here at least were love and loyalty unbounded. I needed look no further for counsel.

"Alma, my princess," I said to her, "as you gave me sage counsel in the palace of Og, swaying the hostile minds of the Yuki chieftains, so give it to me now. What shall I do? Tell me, and I will obey you, for I know not what to do. Tamsa and the chiefs clamor to be led out against Timour. And yet, if we leave our defenses we fight equal in the plain, with the issue doubtful. Whereas, if we delay, and secure ourselves here, Timour must attack or see his army melt away, for a rebel's strength lies in action, and not in tarrying.

"It would be my own plan, then, to wait, since I hold the ford, and supplies can reach us freely from the ships. Yet, if I do so, I fear that my men will fail me. Tamsa wishes me no good, the Yuki and the whites remember their mutual jealousies and wrongs, old Epsilon is with Timour and works on the soldiers' superstitions. What shall I do? Decide, O my princess, for yours is the realm, and I am but one who loves you."

"I will answer thee, my dear lord," she replied, "out of my heart, as it is given to me to see this matter. Since there is disaffection within thy ranks and sedition in Nork, since Kara marches with her fresh troops to join Timour, lead out thine army against him the morrow morn, and let the issue of the morrow's battle settle the fate of the realms of the Yuki—aye, and my people's, too, and our own."

Her eyes flashed proudly; she drew herself out of my arms, and stood up, a commanding figure in the little tent.

"Fight, then, and delay not, Ruuf," she said. "For with your victory all is won, and to-morrow's night shall see Timour dead or captive, or flying, a beaten man, into his fastnesses."

CHAPTER XVII

THE TRAP

I WENT OUT of the tent with all my courage restored. And, because Tamsa was still one of my captains, and in charge of a greater number than any Yuki chief, I went to him first to proclaim my intention.

I found him in his tent with the leaders of the house. At my entry they made their obeisance, but the expression on their faces was at once furtive and bitter. I did not doubt that they had been discussing my plans, perhaps plotting to circumvent them.

"I bring thee good news, O Tamsa, and you, O leaders of the Yuki," I said. "At dawn to-morrow our army leaves the plateau to attack Timour."

They looked at one another. Then Khai, who was the most straightforward of all, rose and came up to me.

"Let my lord forgive the bitter words I spoke," he said. "To-morrow's light shall see Khai and his men the foremost in the fight; and if it go against us, Khai will not survive it."

He left the tent, and, seeing that there was no further response, I went out also.

I had decided on my way back to visit a picket, one of five men which I had set on a small knoll just out of sight of the edge of the plateau, and invisible from it. Its purpose was to watch the Yuki camp and report any suspicious movement in it. It had grown dark while I was with Alma, and I had stumbled upon the spot before I discovered that the knoll was abandoned.

As I looked about me, something came across my mouth, dragging me backward. Before I could utter a cry, a gag was thrust into my throat.

Four or five men held me, and in spite of my struggles I was thrown to the ground and pinioned. Something was thrust into my nostrils—some potent drug that made my head swim. I grew faint. I ceased to struggle; through the haze before my eyes I was only dimly conscious of the faces looking into my own. But I recognized them: two were those of the two guards who had accompanied Tamsa in the tunnel, the third was the face of old Epsilon.

I was dimly conscious of being lifted upon the shoulders of the pair and carried down the hill. I strove to struggle, but my limbs seemed to have been deprived of the power of movement. At the foot of the hill I was placed upon the back of a horse; there followed a short journey, the sense of being laid upon a couch then blankness.

It could not have lasted long, for when I opened my eyes again I saw a single star shining through the flap of a tent. Beneath it, grim in the light of the quarter-moon, was the plateau, with its camp-fires, and the tent over which it hung radiantly I knew for Alma's.

Deep silence everywhere, and Alma ignorant of what had befallen me! I struggled again to move, and found that the power of the drug was evanescent, for I could already move my limbs slightly. As I stirred I heard the sweep of a woman's robe behind me. With difficulty I turned my head to look.

I was in a tent with Kara!

It was equipped with all the barbaric splendor of the Yuki. There were gold and jade ornaments, a sword studded with gems, a suit of white armor which Kara had put off, fashioned of silver welded on steel; it was the tent of an Amazon, but Kara had put off the Amazon with her armor.

She stood before me, attired in her royal robes, with a light coronet of gold upon her head. Her slumberous eyes were fixed intently on mine. "Have no fear, Ruuf, son of Og," she said, "for Kara does not stoop to murder. Moreover, the pledge I made thee in the audience hall was true, though not for Alma, who has ever hated me and kept me down."

I succeeded with difficulty in raising myself into a sitting posture upon the couch. Kara placed a pillow of soft silk beneath my head, and seated herself beside me.

"Neither does Kara hold Ruuf, the son of Og, a prisoner against his will," she continued. "I had a message to deliver to you, and there was no other way to bring you to me, for I know that Ruuf would never trust himself in Kara's hands despite her pledge to him."

The weakness that overcame me held me as if in chains. I lay back on the pillow, listening helplessly.

"Epsilon's drug is potent, but in an hour its effect will be gone," said Kara. "So we will talk together, and afterward, if Kara's proposals do not find favor with you, you shall return to your camp unharmed. Kara pledges her word. But if Timour knew, assuredly he would not be satisfied with any mild revenge. So, being in Kara's power, trust you her word!"

This was logical with a vengeance. The princess smiled, and, raising my hand, which had fallen limp on the silken covering, took it between her own.

"I called you the son of Og, O Ruuf," she said, "and I know, as Timour knows, that you are Og's son. So, being in truth a Yuki, and brought up to manhood among your own people, even if among the humble, what madness ailed you that you spurned Kara and brought woes such as these upon the land?

"Was it love of Alma, my half-sister? Verily, she is false, as you think me false. Do you not know that she is affianced to our kinsman Tamsa, and practices state-craft to use you against Timour and, later, against Og, our protector?

"I say this freely, for I do not love you. I am too proud to love one who has put me to open shame. Yet I will be your queen, for Timour's sake, that he may unite all factions among the

Yuki and whites by our marriage, and, ruling this land, make you tributary prince of Nork. What say you, O Ruuf?"

I said nothing. Assuredly some dreadful power had been in the drug that Epsilon had given me, for my past memories, which had always been with me, not indeed as memories, but as a subconscious force, guiding my motives, vanished completely.

At Kara's words I had felt myself once again thrill with the pride of the Yuki blood, as that first morning in the cave when Malachi showed me my face in the water-bowl. And truth, and honor, even my love grew weak under the influence of this soul-racking potion.

I loved Alma, but only as the Yuki loved. I saw her no longer as my love through innumerable ages. And the wild hopes that had possessed me when first I learned of my birth and prospects filled me again. Here was my empire, ready to my hand, for my betrayal of Alma's cause would disintegrate our army and give me a bloodless victory.

I felt my shame as something foreign, forced into my heart by the drug that had been given me. I felt as if it was another personality whose heart was filled with treachery, as if I, who loved Alma immutably, was something apart from this scheming Yuki prince wrestling with his plots on the couch.

"Surely none but a madman would refuse Kara's offer," the girl pursued. "And afterward—who knows if love may not grow between us? Ah, why should I lie to thee, O Ruuf?" she went on, springing to her feet and facing me with flashing eyes. "I love thee, as I never thought to love, for Kara knows her lord, as every woman must some time, and none but Ruuf has scorned her!"

She fell upon her knees beside me, and looked into my face. I felt her fingers fumbling at my girdle. And, powerless to resist her, I saw her draw out of my pouch the little vial that Alma had given me.

"This gift, O Ruuf, shall make us both immortal," she continued. "To-night we will depart for Nork, there to be wedded by the priests of the Buddha. There we shall hold our court together, and Timour, seeing thee Kara's husband, will put his wrath away, and when the time is propitious we shall supplant him. Speak to me, beloved, for I can feign hate no longer."

I saw the vial in her hands without emotion. I saw her slip it into her robes. I was indifferent to the stupefied man on the couch, yielding to Kara's spell.

And then I saw the star again, through the opening of the tent. And, with a rush, my two parts united. Again I was Ruuf, son of Og, but bearing his submerged and guiding memories. It hung like a pure beacon light above Alma, sleeping in her tent, sure of my faith—Alma, from whom my own heart had never wandered.

I struggled up, pushing Kara aside. I saw the changed look on her face; yet she did not rise, but remained kneeling beside me, a smile upon her lips and wild hate on her face.

There sounded a rustle at the tent door. I saw the flap lifted back. Before me stood Epsilon, behind him Tamsa, and, staring at me with dilated, horror-filled eyes, Alma.

Her presence drove the stupefying effects of the drug from my brain. I sprang to my feet. I ran toward her and recoiled before her unflinching coldness.

"Alma, hear me!" I cried, as the look on Tamsa's face betrayed the trick. "By your love, listen to me!"

She turned to Tamsa.

"Speak for us, O Tamsa," she said.

"Harken, O Ruuf!" began Tamsa caustically. "This is a situation that requires explaining, though you and I know well how it came about. But now I speak for the Princess Alma, who is not so versed in conspiracies as you and I.

"It is not an hour since Epsilon here came into our camp, under a flag of truce, to announce that you had gone to the Princess Kara to ask her to intercede with Timour and make a peace that would save your life and give you a subsidiary kingdom. He offered us safe conduct here, that we might accompany him and learn the truth, pledging himself by the sacred symbol of the Buddha, which has never been turned to treacherous use.

"Now listen further! When in the council hall you refused to attack Timour, many among the Yuki nobles called you a traitor. And these murmurs broke out afresh when you camped here, against the plan that had been made, and again when you were unwilling to fight. Yet for the sake of our cause I saved you from deposition, alleging that you were faithful.

"All these things I told the Princess Alma, in accordance with my duty; but she, like a woman, clung with all her heart to the man who called himself her lover; nor would she believe even when Epsilon came to us. It was not until your tent had been searched for you and found empty that she consented to come; and then only that she might prove you true. Now she has seen. What say you, O princess?" he asked.

"That the heart speaks, and may be deceived, but the eyes see and cannot be deceived," she answered in a low voice.

I ran to her, pushing Tamsa aside. I clasped her hands. I felt them tremble in mine. I knew that I could regain her. My looks must have convinced her, for she asked in agitation:

"If you would have me believe, tell me, O Ruuf, where is the vial I gave you?"

I FELT, rather than saw, Kara smile. I put my hand to my girdle pouch and found it empty. I swung upon Kara, and saw old Epsilon slip from the tent.

Horrified, I stared into Alma's eyes and saw the light die out in them.

"Let us return, O Tamsa, my kinsman," she said gravely, "for day is not far away, and there will be a heavy morrow for us. Much blood will flow, and many brave men will fall; but, whether we fall or conquer, one name shall never again be spoken, either when I reign queen in Nork or when I wander beyond the icy river whose waters bring oblivion. O Tamsa—"

She broke off and addressed Kara.

"This is an ill deed that thou has done," she said. "Henceforth there shall never be peace between us."

"Yet, seeing that Timour's victory is sure, and that Timour is a merciful prince, for what wouldst thou still fight, my sister?" Kara asked.

"Call me never sister again," said Alma. "And, as for what I fight for, let it be said that it is for the memory of one who has died."

I saw consternation on Tamsa's face.

"Surely there need be no war, O Alma!" he cried. "For, with the unmasking of this conspiracy, all cause for war has gone."

"O Tamsa, lead mine hosts!" answered the girl decisively, using the Yuki formula which permits no reply.

And they were gone, and I turned to where Kara stood, a mocking figure beside the silken couch.

"A royal part!" I cried in scorn.

"A part that is played and ended," she answered with disdain. "Go forth, O Ruuf, the swineherd's son, for Kara keeps her word, and you are free to depart. Only see that you fall not into Timour's hand."

And, flinging up her arms, she added with passionate emphasis:

"Did you think in your infatuation that Kara's love could stoop to such a base-born clown, or even to one of royal blood who had put Kara to shame before the nobles of the Yuki? Go, and be glad that Kara's vengeance leaves you whole. Go forth, cast out by all, back to the swineherd's hut—for Kara keeps her honor and repays her foes!"

CHAPTER XVIII

MALACHI SPEAKS

I WENT OUT of the tent blindly. Two Yuki guards, who were posted in front of it, and had evidently received their instructions, conducted me by a long detour around their lines toward the river. Sometimes a sentry's challenge drew the countersign from them, but otherwise our journey was a silent one.

They led me to the ford of the river, and indicated that I was to cross, but did not enter the stream. They stood upon the bank, watching me. When I was on the other side they departed, and I climbed the shelving bank and sat down desolate among the trees.

I was too stunned, for a long time to be able to think, but after a while the situation built itself up in my mind in this manner:

Tamsa, who had coveted the throne, had been infuriated by my appearance upon the scene in the guise of the deliverer. The war with Timour had recast the political situation, and he had planned to rid himself of me by murder and assume my place. But, balked in this scheme, as also by Alma's unexpected arrival in the camp, he must have contrived to carry out an earlier plan made with Epsilon, whereby, through Kara's treachery, I was to be so discredited in Alma's eyes that my deposition was an almost automatic consequence.

That would give him all he desired. And I had no doubt that Alma's decision to fight on the morrow had all but wrecked his plans.

What would he do? But what could I do? Madly as I longed to strike a blow against Timour, I could see that my appearance in the Yuki camp would disrupt our forces and bring Alma defeat, captivity, and shame; for the archers were all for me, as were numbers of Og's body-guard, who saw in me only the heir to the Yuki throne.

For Alma's sake I must play no part in the events of the morrow. I must remain a spectator of the fight till its conclusion. If Alma lost, I meant to fling myself into the defeated ranks and find death among them: but if she won I must go back to my swineherd's cabin and bear my intolerable shame, as Kara had told me.

I FLUNG myself down among the bushes, and so fatigued was I that I think I must have slept a little, in spite of my agony of mind, for suddenly I started up at the sound of some one coming along the track toward me, and hardly knew where I was for the moment.

Staff in hand, approaching me, was old Malachi. He stood before me, his wrists linked by his golden chain, looking at me benignantly, and wagging his white beard.

"Greeting, O Ruuf, son of Og!" he began ironically. "How comes it that the deliverer of the captive people and heir to the Yuki Empire wanders alone here, when the battle is set for dawn and he should be among his hosts?"

"Because I have been betrayed by those in whom I trusted, O Malachi," I answered.

"And behold," he continued in the same ironic tone, "he has not saved his people, and yet neither has he won the prize he sought!"

"Is mine the blame, O Malachi?" I asked.

"Truly, my son, you yourself have said it," he answered. "The test I gave you was too hard for you, and at the time of the inevitable choice you chose to follow your desires rather than fulfill your mission. Of this I warned you."

"Never in plain speech!" I cried.

"It was not permissible, O Ruuf, for a man must act in ignorance, that he be not swayed from the path on which he sets his feet."

"Tell me this," I cried, standing before the tall old swaying figure and looking into the hoary eyes, which were fixed on mine, not unkindly. "Why was it wrong of me to seek the happiness that came to me, yet right for me to sacrifice myself for a cause unknown to me?"

"O Ruuf, you do not understand the ways of fate," he answered, "nor yet the task that is set unto each one of us at birth. With the dim sight which long study had given me, I foresaw that only by renunciation could you work out the duty that had been laid on you. You declined it—and lo, you wander outcast, having lost both things and gained nothing!

"Had you not sought your happiness with the Princess Alma," he said, "Tamsa had held true to his faith, and even now Timour would kneel in supplication before you."

"And now?" I asked.

"There is still a choice, O Ruuf. You are free to go back to your swineherd's hut and live out your days there in peace."

"Or—"

"Or end the course on which you have begun, which is the better way, knowing that, though you shall lose your heart's desire, at the end all shall be well. For you have won the prize and lost the prize, and yet shall win the prize again, though not in the way you hope. And in the course of time another deliverer shall be raised up to us, who shall purge this land of the Yuki, and things shall be as in the long ago, when the wise white men builded Nork."

I gripped the old man by the arm.

"You tell me that I shall win the prize again, though not in the way I hope!" I cried. "And these are the words that you spoke to me in the pit."

"Even so, Ruuf, son of Og, for even then I foresaw, though dimly, your inevitable failure. Verily, in the end you shall have your heart's desire; yet, if you knew in what manner, it would appear unattainable. For first you must pass through a realm where even in dreams no memory of the Princess Alma will come to you."

"Show me the way, and I will go there at once, and suffer all, so long as I win her in the end!" I cried.

"The place is very far away," he answered.

"You speak of death," I retorted.

"Not death," he answered, "but rather life that never ceases— for never was I not, nor thou, nor shall we ever cease to be."

Where had I heard that said before? Who was it that had told me this in days gone by?

"Beyond that place," continued Malachi, "perchance we shall be together again, under a kindlier destiny. For my task here is ended, and there, it may be, I shall be a slave no longer, and a healer of ills, rather than a prophet of them. And by a sign that I shall give you, you will remember me, and know that you hold the prize after all, and regain your memories. This, then, shall be the sign. I shall ask you, not knowing why I ask it, and myself remembering nothing—for such is my desire; I shall ask you if you are happy to have made the sacrifice."

"My decision is made," I answered. "Let me win the prize in the end, however hard and long the way, rather than lose it and go back to my swineherd's hut, and live in peace."

"You have chosen wisely," answered Malachi. "Gird yourself, then, to play the man when it shall be required of you!"

And suddenly I saw Malachi no longer.

I found myself kneeling on the wet ground across the river. My memory of the night's scene rushed back to me, but no longer with the same poignancy. A veil seemed to have been drawn across my past; I had erred, but all might yet be won.

And yet I was not sure whether I had seen Malachi or only dreamed of him. I knew that the old man was in the habit of wandering alone throughout the country regions, where he was well treated by the peasantry, who regarded him as one inspired.

It might have been a vision, or he might have bound me to my task anew. But, whichever it had been, I despaired no longer.

And, passively, I awaited what was to come, feeling myself a pawn in the hands of destiny.

I waited for the dawn. It came quickly, in crimson and gray, a fiery sun that sent his burning arrows from behind great storm clouds packed on the horizon. As if in foreknowledge of what was to be, the carrion vultures hung, high in the sky, and soared above the battle-field.

Presently there reached my ears a distant hum from either camp as the two armies wakened. The camp-fires smoldered, sending up high columns of smoke, under the drizzling rain that had begun to fall. A fine day for Halkh's archers! I felt my spirits rise as I thought that fate was not playing into Timour's hands in this regard, at least.

The neigh of horses intermingled with the clatter of shields. The sun appeared for a moment behind the clouds, and I saw the ridge and the plateau black with men, standing to arms. Across the stream the horses, which had been led to the bank to drink, were being saddled.

Then my hopes went down with a rush. For, looking across to Timour's lines, I saw an army half as many again, lining the further edge of the crest; and I realized the difficulty of the task before Alma's men that day.

It was the reenforcements which Kara had brought to Timour from among the disloyal followers of Og. I saw them with despair, praying with all my soul that Tamsa, false in all other things, would at least prove true in the fight.

CHAPTER XIX

THE BATTLE

HARDLY HAD OUR horsemen gained their saddles when Timour's cavalry advanced in line to meet them.

They formed to meet the charge and advanced at a trot which changed to a gallop. Swords flashed, and, with a mighty shock, the two lines came together.

Dust rose in swirls, tipped with the flashing points of swords. I heard the commands of captains, the oaths and shrieks of the combatants; and from both watching armies a mighty cheer uprose. Again, as if by physical tension, I prayed that Tamsa would hold true.

Suddenly, out of the dust, riderless horses began to break back toward Timour's lines; then horses that carried reeling riders; then the dust settled, disclosing our men in hot pursuit, and Timour's horsemen flying in disarray, over a ground littered with dead.

We followed them right to their lines, until the arrows began to fall; then my horse withdrew and resumed their place by the river.

Yells from the plateau greeted this spectacle answering shouts came from the camp of Timour, and, breaking through the compact lines of his legionaries the archers and slingers advanced at the double. They halted fifty yards from the plateau and shot their missiles.

But from the plateau came such an answering shower of arrows, shot by Halkh's famous archers, that, unable to beat down their fire, Timour's bowmen and slingers retreated with hot haste, leaving their dead behind them, amounting to nearly a fourth of their number.

But Timour's ranks opened to receive them, and then, with a single and simultaneous movement, his whole twelve hundred heavy-armed troops advanced slowly across the valley, their yataghans waving, their shields all in line, like huge flowers, upon their arms.

The sight was the most superb that I have ever seen. This was the largest and best drilled body of swordsmen that had ever been raised among the Yuki. Many were Og's own men, who had deserted him to follow what they considered the rising star of Timour. Trained from youth to contempt of death, they moved forward at a quick walk, which changed to a slow run as they approached the plateau.

The storm of arrows met them, but their armor protected them, and few fell. The little gaps in their ranks were at once closed with mathematical precision. They were within twenty paces when suddenly I saw a movement among Alma's men, and a chief whom I thought to be Khai sprang forward.

With a shout that reached my ears across the valley he ran single-handed down the plateau, and after him, breaking line, the whole eight hundred swept down the hill after him, forfeiting the advantage of their position.

Our archers, unable to fire, grounded their bows. The heavy legionaries, mad with the lust of battle, clashed in frenzied combat. Yuki was pitted against Yuki, and all the pride of clan rivalry, aroused, swept discipline away.

The shock of the collision was as of two waves meeting. In the center the impact threw each side back a yard or two at the onset; and the movement, transferred into a lateral one by the sudden stoppage of momentum, sent out ripples along the lines, flinging out the debris of reeling figures to either wing. The yataghans writhed like serpents above the dust-clouds.

Suddenly the line of Timour's sword-tips grew concave and

broke. For a few moments the two bodies seemed to be mingled. Then, with loud cheers, Alma's men broke through Timour's ranks in solid phalanx; the pennons swayed and went down, and Timour's legionaries were parted like the earth flung up by a plow.

Surely our men would halt and reform their ranks, instead of pressing forward. But even as the instinct of discipline held them for a moment I saw a milk-white banner raised on the plateau, and an armed figure rode forth, accompanied by a small body-guard.

Armored and carrying a light sword, I knew it to be Alma, for none but she could ride beneath that banner. As I watched in wonder and dawning fear I saw her gallop down-hill to join her legionaries, and with triumphant shouts they clustered round her and swept her forward with them.

I was mad with desire to play my part, and yet I dared do nothing. I followed Alma with my eyes, hoping, praying, raving when the dust hid her, breathing when she emerged.

Sullenly fighting, Timour's heavy-armed troops withdrew, leaving between their flanks the gap which our men had made; thus his lines resembled a huge, broken bow, extending in a semicircle about the plateau. And now, if ever, was the moment when rashness might be retrieved and victory gained.

For, pinned down by our attack upon his center, Timour's repulse could be converted into rout by Tamsa, if he flung his light-armed forces upon his flank.

Then the full significance of Tamsa's treachery came home to me, and blacker than I had conceived it.

For, instead of moving forward in echelon, as I had bidden him, Tamsa wheeled his column about, and the whole regiment started for Timour's camp, with the obvious intention of going over to him, moving with flying flags out of range of the combat, and laying our whole right center open to the enemy.

Instantly, with loud cries, the Yuki companies on Timour's left swept past them and surged into the breach that he had made, racing for the plateau, protected only by our little force of archers.

So sudden was their onset that these had hardly time to fit arrows to their bowstrings when the Yuki were among them, hacking them down with their curved yataghans. In less than two minutes the dreadful scene was ended. The archers died where they had stood, their bodies heaped the plateau, and Timour's men, in possession of our camp, completely encircled Alma's, cutting them off from their base.

Meanwhile our horse beside the ford, having repelled Timour's, remained there in sullen inaction. I knew that the same treacherous influences had been at work among them, and, though they did not go over to Timour nor leave the field, they had evidently no intention of taking further part in the battle.

Then, even as Alma's legionaries pressed forward, I saw banners upraised behind the crest, and Kara's fresh army, cheering wildly, swept forward to fill the breach. As they ran, without checking their pace they swiftly converted their formation into that of a wedge-shaped phalanx. They hurled themselves on Alma's men: at the same time Timour's legions closed in upon their flanks once more.

Like a vortex, our men seemed to suck in Timour's on every side. They were fighting back to back now, barely five hundred strong, assuming the form of a ring, which sometimes lengthened into an ellipse, but, though contracting momentarily, was never broken.

They were trying to regain the plateau, and in intervals between the assaults moved slowly backward. Again and again the storm broke on them—broke and withdrew, like waves on granite.

I could bear the sight no longer. I scrambled into the stream, reached the far side of the ford, found a riderless horse drinking there, leaped on his back, and spurred him toward our sullen horsemen. They knew me and surrounded me with menacing gestures. What wild words I uttered I do not recall, but of a sudden cheers broke out, and a few moments later I found myself at their head, thundering across the valley toward Alma and her men at bay.

Timour's and Kara's legions had closed about the little army, almost concealing them from sight. They filled the valley, and so great was the press that they seemed like a flowing, molten mass, whose center constantly spewed out dead men, flinging them up as from the crater of a volcano.

Detaching themselves from the fight, two companies of Timour's men advanced to meet us. We were among them, bearing them back, and now riders and footmen were mingled inextricably upon the plain.

I saw the milk-white banner of Alma in the distance, opposite it, not far away, Kara's of white and yellow, and the clash of armed men between those two storm-centers of the battle. I strove to cleave a passage toward them. But suddenly, through the furious rain-storm that swept the valley, the yellow pennon of Timour was upraised before my eyes, with Timour under it.

He saw me, and, with a shout, he sprang toward me. An archer at his side curved his long bow, and the shaft pierced through my horse's heart. It reared and fell, sending me clattering in my heavy mail at Timour's feet.

He whirled his yataghan; and then, as I tried to rise, before it had fallen, a man leaped with a shout between us. It was Khai, and Timour's blade clove him from throat to waist. He reeled, and looked at me with blazing eyes.

"Ah, my lord, Khai is ever loyal!" he mumbled, and fell dead at Timour's feet.

I rushed at Timour. Our swords clashed on each other's shields. As we fought hand to hand in the thick of the press those round us paused to watch us.

"Come to me, O swineherd's son," roared Timour. "Here we stand face to face like men, and not mock-combatants on mare-back. Come, and I will give thy body to feast the carrion vultures!"

He swung a fearful blow at my head. I parried it, but his yataghan slipped over my steel and shore clean through the iron crest above my helmet. I struck with all my force against his breast. The point glided over the smooth armor, and the hilt of the sword, catching him under the chin, sent him staggering back.

He ran at me, sword in his right hand, a short dagger in his left. Beneath his furious onset I was forced to give ground. But suddenly his attack ceased. He stared at me as a man in a dream, and I, in turn, looking at him in wonder, forbore to take advantage.

"Is it you, Basil?" he muttered. "Who are you, and how came you here? Where is—"

The legionaries pressed between us. In a moment Timour's yellow banner had been borne far away, dipping and rising over the locked hosts.

And that is the last clear picture that I have of the battle. For a thick fog came sweeping down the valley, blotting out friend from foe. With the roar of the fight about me, the hoofs upraised, the flash of blades and clanging of shields, I fought my way toward the place where I had seen Alma's banner.

I beat off blows from unseen enemies, I cleared a passage, and, just as I had grown hopeless, I saw the milk-white flag flutter from among a little cluster of men, all that now remained of the host whom I had led out to battle. About them was a parapet of dead, and among them, on foot, was Alma.

With the sudden surge of a tidal wave a line of horsemen came out of the fog and hurled themselves against us. Heading them I saw Tamsa. I strove to reach him, but, pinned helpless among the struggling mass, I could not. And I saw him and lost him, and saw Alma and lost her again, as the fog wreaths played about me.

As the press of battle swept from me again I saw a horse at

my side, dragging its dead rider, who, caught in the stirrup by his spur, hung face downward in the red mud churned up by Tamsa's raid. I tore the clod from the iron and mounted. The sounds about me were growing less. I looked about for Alma's banner, but could not find it. I seemed alone on that vast field of slaughter.

Then suddenly, as the fog lifted momentarily, I saw Tamsa and Alma riding side by side, not a stone's throw from me.

CHAPTER XX

TAMSA

AND, EVEN AS I looked, the fog closed down again.

I dashed toward them, but encountered nothing. I rode back, shouting, and the fog, like a high wall, caught up the reverberating echoes of my voice in mocking tones. I rode in circles, swathed in the drip of the mist, and never a soul I saw upon the battle-field.

Around me I still heard the cries of victory, the groans of the wounded, but I seemed like a man under a spell, for I was alone, wherever I rode. At length, hopelessly lost, I drew rein, waiting for the fog to clear.

I knew the fight was lost, and that none of our loyal men survived—none, except myself, branded thus with the shame of Tamsa's traitors.

Timour and Tamsa had won everything. I pictured Alma's fate, and again I rode helplessly in the fog, now hearing no sounds at all; and again I halted.

I tied the reins about the stump of a tree that loomed out of the mist, and lay down on the dripping ground. For an hour, at least, I lay there, hearing nothing except the cawing of vast flocks of crows, calling each other to their feast.

Then of a sudden the western sun burst through the clouds, rolling up the mists, and revealing my position and the panorama about me.

In some manner I had strayed to one of the camel-tracks that led into the hills, and my horse, following it, had carried

140

me to the summit, which was not high. Beneath me was a vast track of flat country, extending from shore to shore of Baruk-Halin.

Far away was the battle-field, with patches of black upon its verdure where the heaped up bodies of the dead disclosed the centers of the contest, and in one place was a great mound, where Alma's legionaries had died to a man and never yielded.

Circling above them were the crows and vultures, still fearing to swoop till all grew still. Horses were browsing peaceably along the river's edge. On the ridge were the black tents of Timour's army, fronted by ours on the plateau, now the spoil of the enemy. I saw the white and yellow banner of Kara, and the four yellow pennons of Timour flying free from the four corners of his own tent.

And then, lifting up my eyes, I saw, clear against the sun, Alma and Tamsa riding a great distance away.

The sight drove the blood to my head. Cunning and rage together took hold of me. I galloped along the track toward the point for which they seemed to be heading—a cove among some steep cliffs on the north shore of Baruk-Halin, beyond which I could see the arm of the sea, and the hills of outlying Nork upon the other side.

I calculated that the road I traversed would enable me to cut off their flight just before they approached the cove, and I was right in this calculation. An hour later I spurred my panting horse into a clump of bushes and, sword in hand, waited there.

I heard the tramp of their horses: then they drew rein not twenty paces from me and, hidden as I was among the trees, did not suspect my presence.

"The way is long, and I am very tired, O Tamsa," said Alma wearily.

"Have courage, O Alma," answered Tamsa, "for it is not far to the refuge of which I spoke, once we have crossed the channel. There you shall rest to-night, and to-morrow we shall continue on our way. Though Timour capture Nork, owing to the treachery of that swineherd's son, better to carve out our kingdom at the head of my legions than to rule under him."

I gasped as he uttered the words. No longer satisfied to keep his evil compact with Timour, I guessed that he was planning to make for the tributary lands and raise an army for his overthrow.

"I know nothing of that," answered the girl, "and I seem to care nothing. Would that Ruuf had been true to me!"

"Would that he had! But he was an impostor, fishing in the troubled waters of politics, O princess, and had not wit enough to play even that part truly, but must needs have betrayed us. You saw him in Kara's tent; you do not believe in him?"

"My heart cannot convince me," she replied, "and yet I know he could not have gone there except for treachery."

"Bad enough," said Tamsa, "but think of the brave men who lie dead on the field because of his double treachery in the fight!"

"Of that I could see nothing, O Tamsa."

"Yet it was plain to us upon the plateau. For at the moment when your charge had assured the day to us Ruuf fled from the field, carrying my regiment with him. But even in their flight they cast him out; and I saw him pierced through the back, as he ran, by a Yuki swordsman."

I heard her sob, but she returned no answer.

"Surely that traitor is nothing to you, O Alma," persisted Tamsa. "When you reign with me, queen over Nork—"

Looking through the leaves I saw her start. "That, O Tamsa, can never be," she answered. "Have I not told you so?"

"Whom then should the Princess Alma wed, if not Tamsa, her kinsman?" he demanded indignantly.

"O Tamsa, if this indeed was the purpose of your rescue of me, rather would I have died among my men at Timour's hands," she answered.

"This, indeed, was my purpose," said Tamsa blandly. "For without you, my ambition dies. So, O kinswoman, whom I have ever loved, Tamsa unveils his heart and tells you that you are in his power. Further, I will reveal this to you—a bargain was made between myself and Kara, whereby Ruuf, the impostor, was to be overthrown. Kara would become Timour's bride, while you and I would reign together in Nork. If, now, I have changed my plans, it is because my regiment waits for me by the river, to move on Nork before Timour suspects my purpose. There I shall overthrow King Og, as I overthrew the fool Ruuf, who went to his doom this day, by my maneuver."

I saw the girl recoil from him in horror at his words.

"And Ruuf in Kara's tent?" she gasped.

"He, too, had his own schemes," he answered lightly, "but mine succeeded while his failed. Therefore, since we both schemed for love of you and for the crown, choose the better man, O Alma!"

She clasped her hands piteously together.

"O Ruuf," she said solemnly, "if indeed thou be in the realms of the dead, and yet not wholly beyond the river of forgetfulness, I tell thee that I love thee and shall never be Tamsa's bride. Aid me, if thou art able!"

At her words I touched my horse's flank and rode out into the track.

Alma started and screamed; the look on Tamsa's face turned from cunning to fear.

"Fight thy last fight, O traitor!" I cried, and rode at him.

He pulled his sword reluctantly out of its sheath and galloped to meet me. Even as I rode I saw the foreknowledge of death on Tamsa's face. I caught his wild blow on my shield and pierced him through beneath the breast-plate.

He reeled and fell, and writhed upon the ground.

Alma ran to his side and, kneeling, began unbuckling his armor. She tried to stanch the flowing blood with her silken robes. But a glance at Tamsa's face showed that he would betray no one any more.

"Forgive!" he whispered to both of us.

"Say, then, how I came into the tent of Kara!" I cried, still raging, and standing over us with my sword at his throat—though I could not have struck again.

"Ruuf, thou wast guiltless," he whispered back. "It was Epsilon and my men who gagged and bound and carried thee there, as had been planned between us."

"O Tamsa, kinsman, how earnest thou to betray the cause we loved, to which we were both pledged from childhood?" wept Alma.

"For love of thee," he answered in a voice so low that it hardly reached our ears. "I have erred greatly; yet perchance when I am born again, if thou be living, O Alma, I shall requite thee."

His hands sought the Buddhic rosary about his neck, and he strung his beads round his fingers, muttering. Suddenly he opened his eyes and looked at me.

"All is not lost," he whispered. "Go to Nork, win my men; hold Timour at bay. Forgive me, Ruuf, whom I have wronged!"

I held his hands, and in a moment the light went out of his eyes.

Alma kneeled beside his body, weeping bitterly. When at last she grew composed, I drew her to me.

"Alma," I said, "I have slain him, but in a fair fight, and to save thee. What is to be between us?"

"Ah, Ruuf, my lord, how couldst thou have done otherwise?" she answered. "If it be in thy heart to let me go, I will find refuge in some land where I shall never trouble thee again."

"I will go with thee, Alma."

"With me, my lord?" Her voice was tremulous. "But I—unworthy—faithless—" she sobbed, and broke down. Then, as her courage reasserted itself:

"O my lord, if indeed thou canst forgive, Alma will play her part until the end. So I will ride toward Nork with thee; and if haply we fall beside the road, well; and, if we reach Nork, we shall withstand Timour there."

So we left Tamsa where he had died and rode back toward the river.

CHAPTER XXI

ALMA'S DEFIANCE

WE CAST OUR armor away and rode all night, halting only to rest our horses for brief intervals. On and on we went, skirting the watch-fires that burned round about us, while we reeled in the saddle from want of sleep, and sometimes Alma slept in my arms, lying back against me, our horses stumbling forward, flank by flank. And at last, in the gray of the dawn, we reached the river.

And there, beached on the shore, we saw all that was left of Khom's war-vessels.

Later I was to learn how Timour's navy had fallen upon our weaker one, even while the fight in the valley raged and, after a hard fight, destroyed it, the brave old Khom falling on the deck of the last ship that remained afloat, pierced by six arrows. Timour's ships—the few that remained after the battle—had withdrawn along shore, foundering by the way, until only five made their harbor.

If we had had any hopes, this fresh disaster quenched them. But we searched until we found a navigable boat, stranded beside a hulk, and I rowed Alma across the river, turning back our horses first to become the property of any who found them.

We traveled into Nork along a deserted countryside. But when we reached the city gates we found a straggling multitude of peasantry waiting before them, in terror of the victors' wrath; and presently we were admitted, and, passing through the streets unrecognized—for Alma's rain-soaked silken robes hung round her like any peasant woman's garments—we reached the bronze gates of the palace.

At sight of me the archers on guard stared incredulously; then their shouts were taken up through the courts and presently Halkh came running and saw us there, and, as the gates swung back, he kneeled before us, kissing my hand and Alma's.

"My lord and princess, we thought you dead!" he cried. "Evil is the news that reaches us, hour by hour. Khom is dead and his ships sunk, and rumor tells us that none of the army that went out survives—not one. Yea, lord, we thought you dead, and, as for the Princess Alma, we believed that Timour had seized her as the prize of victory, if she had escaped the slaughter. Ah, my lord, pardon me that I permitted her to depart secretly, for had she fallen I should have embraced my sword!"

Which was the oblique Yuki phrase for suicide. The chieftain was almost incoherent with joy. I understood the strength of the loyalty which had held him back from such a needless sacrifice until the report of our death had been verified.

Then I acquainted him, as quickly and as briefly as possible, with the story of the battle and of Tamsa's treachery. When the archers learned of the massacre of their comrades they raised such a shout of wrath that it was with difficulty they could be restrained from rushing out of the palace to begin an indiscriminate slaughter of the white populace.

But Halkh managed to send them about their duties, and when Alma, half-dead from need of sleep, had gone to her maidens, I drew Halkh aside.

"Against them we have your fifty archers and possibly a score of men-at-arms from among Og's guard, who can be trusted. Let us consider what it is possible to do. But first tell me of Og. Has he learned anything of our defeat?"

"Nay, lord," answered Halkh. "Since your departure he has not left his audience-hall. Ever he drinks and feasts or sleeps on his throne, and he recounts his victories of years ago and boasts of his intention to join you and conquer Timour. And none has dared acquaint him with the truth."

"Then let him not be told," I answered. "And watch his audience-hall, and when any of his fellow-revelers leaves it, seize him and place him where he can do no harm."

"That is done now, my lord," answered Halkh, meaning that my command should be obeyed promptly.

He called two of his archers, trusted followers, and gave them my order. I watched them depart upon their mission.

"Now tell me of the feint by the bridge and how it failed," I continued.

"My lord, there is little to tell save this: Hardly had the oxen crossed the bridge, the ships meanwhile making a demonstration against it, than Timour's captain, as if knowing of the trick, opened his gates, and in rushed the herd, whereon the gates were closed. Nor did he answer Khom's challenge. So it all went for nought, and this is not strange, seeing that half those in the palace are traitors."

He paused, and looked about him carefully before continuing.

"Now, to speak plainly between us, O my Lord Ruuf, if Timour lays seize to us it is only a question of days before he and his ships force the bridge, or before his heavy rams come up to breach our gates; and as for Nork, it is his for the entering of it."

"The people will flock to his banners, O Halkh?" I asked.

"Beyond a doubt, lord, for they fear for their lives. As yet there is no knowledge of the magnitude of the disaster. Moreover, it is linked in their minds with the defeat of Khom's ships beyond the rapids, as if the two had been a single battle. And the sight of Timour's five hulks, all that were left of his great navy, battered by the great naval slings, and burned by our fireballs, reeling into his harbor, has created the belief that Timour's victory was by the narrowest of margins. But when the full news is known Nork will acclaim his entry."

"I have been planning this whole night past, O Halkh," I said. "Tell me how long it will require for the tributary princes who are loyal to Og to reach us with their armies."

Halkh thought for a few moments.

"Within five days Prince Chun, of Kaniak-tekat, can bring a thousand warriors before Nork," he answered. "And, five days afterward, if they march swiftly, another thousand can be here under Prince Kang, of Ba-setuna. Both these princes are faithful and can be depended on."

"You can hold out ten days?"

Halkh smiled. "I can but try, or fall trying, my Lord Ruuf," he answered. "Yet, unless Timour can bring his rams against our gates before the princes come, I think we can withstand him."

"Then let messengers on swift horses be despatched to the princes immediately," I said. "And look to it that the keep and the gates be held against Timour until our relief arrives."

"That is done now, my lord," he answered again.

Within ten minutes messengers were speeding northward to the princes, to summon aid; and now, leaving the charge of the palace in Halkh's hands, I went to my apartments. The palace corridors were packed with frightened pages watching the corridor that led into Og's audience-hall; but from behind the hanging carpet there came only the shrill sounds of the fifes, as the deaf and blind fife-players played on, ignorant of all the changes in the land.

I flung myself upon a couch, worn out with weariness—and yet I was too tired to sleep, and my mind took up its problem. Had I acted for the best? The alternative would have been to have sent Alma away secretly, hoping that she could escape Timour. But I had little hope of that. And though he must now have the vial, I believed that he would never rest until he had Alma also, either to hold her as a subsidiary wife to Kara, or for a hostage—or for revenge.

At last, just when I had closed my eyes and the affairs of

state had become a confused, discordant jangle in my mind, there came a knocking at the door. I started up and opened to one of the black pages.

"My Lord Ruuf, will you go into the court?" he stammered, looking at me in terror.

I heard a mighty clamor in the streets. I ran down into the court. Through the bronze gates, at which the archers stood lined, with arrows to their bows, I saw a vast multitude, and posted upon the crests of the ruins opposite the ancient siege ground of the palace, just out of arrow range, the vanguard of Timour's army.

The mob was cheering madly—not for us, but for Timour.

Behind our archers was Halkh with a few of the palace attendants, and with them Alma. As I looked toward them the ranks of the mob opened and a herald came striding forward, attired in particolored robes of red and black, symbolical of war and death.

Ten paces outside the gates he halted, and solemnly, according to the Yuki ritual, he shook his wooden sword toward us, holding it hilt upward.

"The words of Timour unto Og, King of Nork," he declaimed. "Yield you to me, together with your treasure and your palace; yield me your wives; yield me the Princess Alma, of the white people; yield to me Ruuf, the swineherd's son, who has stirred up this trouble in this land; yield me your crown and all that is yours, and feast on Timour's bounty in Timour's land of Baruk-Halin all your days! May they be long!"

Before I could confer with Halkh, Alma had advanced toward the archers. I never saw such pride and courage on any woman's face as on hers.

"The words of Og, King of the Yuki, through the mouth of the Princess Alma," she answered. "Let Timour depart hence into his land and presently I will send Ruuf, my son, unto him, with true men and not traitors, to execute my judgment on him, according to my laws!"

With a gesture of insolent defiance the herald shook the wooden sword again, this time point upward, spread out his robes, and strode back to his lines amid the shouts of the populace, hooting and shrieking out against us, and yet scurrying for safety when any of the archers bent his bow menacingly toward them.

Alma came toward me. "Have I spoken for my lord?" she asked.

"Truly and well," I said.

"Let my lord pardon me that I usurped his words, for I feared that my lord, considering me, would offer terms to Timour."

"Henceforward there can be no terms," I answered. "Too deep a river of blood has flowed between us."

And, satisfied that the gates were unassailable, I went down to the keep. Behind the strong stone walls Halkh's men seemed invulnerable. Through the arrow slits I could see Timour's main forces mustering upon the shore opposite.

And all that day our preparations for defense went on. In the pit the armorers struck out arrows from iron. Cattle were slaughtered, watches appointed; meanwhile Og, ignorant of what was passing, feasted and drank in his great audience-hall; and, dominating all else, the shrill sounds of the female fife-players rang through the palace.

CHAPTER XXII

THE LAST STAND

A DOZEN TIMES that night there was the alarm of trumpets, and a demonstration against the gates which kept our men on the alert. It was only when morning came that we realized that these maneuvers were meant merely to tire out our men. The keep and gates were impregnable; the contest was nothing more than a race between the loyal princes and Timour's battering-rams, now supposed to be lumbering slowly across the roads of Baruk-Halin.

I snatched a few minutes with Alma toward noon of the next day and found her supremely confident. Only three of her women remained with her; the rest had fled from the palace at the first news of our defeat.

Mnerma, the decorous, was one of these. Unaware that it was I who had followed her that night along the secret passage, she addressed me freely.

"Lord Ruuf, it would be a terrible thing if our princess were taken by Prince Timour," she said. "To me, love means naught, and never can, for never have I loved, or let any man look upon me with love; yet, since my Lord Ruuf and the princess love each other, I am resolved that their happiness shall come to them."

"A brave resolve, O Mnerma," I answered, smiling. "Yet I think there are others who have made that resolve and yet are doubtful of its accomplishment."

This I said, of course, out of Alma's hearing. Whether her

own confidence was true or feigned, I did not know, but I was inclined to believe that it was assumed, like mine.

"Lord Ruuf, I have only the weakness of a woman," answered the girl, "and yet women, they say, have wits. Lo, there has come into my mind a plan whereby the princess may yet be delivered; and thou also, my lord."

"Reveal it unto me, O Mnerma," I answered mockingly, "and if it succeed thou shalt have thine own weight in gold for a dowry."

"Speak not to me of dowries, lord," she answered, "for dowries mean naught to me, and I desire only to serve my lord and the princess. But as for the plan, pardon me if I reveal it not until the time come."

That was all I could extract from her, and in truth I gave little thought to the matter. The day wore on. From the windows of the palace we could see Timour's men constantly passing through Nork to take up their posts upon the ruins; there was activity across the bridge, but no attack was made until toward nightfall.

Then Halkh sent a hasty message to me that Timour's ships were leaving their anchorage on the Baruk-Halin shore.

I hurried down to the keep and standing at Halkh's side watched the five battered vessels swing slowly on the tide.

What was Timour's purpose? It would be easy enough to land more troops on the shores of Nork, but, since the city was already Timour's, their presence would be of no avail. Og's palace, built high on the ruins, was wholly impregnable, except by the bridge or the north gates.

We were not left long in suspense for, catching the breeze, the ships spread their sails and came directly toward us. We could see their decks packed with soldiery.

Presently a swarm of arrows and stones, discharged upward from bow and sling, began to fall inside the keep.

It was an old maneuver, and not likely to accomplish much.

I had provided Halkh's men with helmets and body-pieces of iron, and the missiles glanced off these harmlessly.

Our archers, on the contrary, did great execution through the arrow-holes on the massed troops and soon Timour's ships were in hot retreat back to their own shore.

"What think you, lord?" asked Halkh, turning to me.

"A feint, even as ours, to wear out our strength," I answered. "Let half the guard sleep while the other half watches."

"It has been done, my lord."

Hardly had he issued the command when there came a new demonstration across the bridge. Pushing before them a wheeled breastwork of iron-bound planks, a body of Timour's troops came forward, carrying ladders and showing every apparent intention of trying to scale the walls.

But at a distance of forty paces Halkh's bowmen picked them off with unerring aim, despite their protection until, abandoning their improvised cover, they fled in haste to their own fortress.

"What think you now, my lord?" asked Halkh.

"That Timour never meant to storm the keep."

"Yea, my lord, but if these feints be to weary us, does he not weary his own men also, and in greater number? See now, my lord!"

And he pointed toward Timour's hulks, which were again putting out of harbor.

The same demonstration was repeated with the same result. And once more the feint was made over the bridge.

Satisfied that no danger was threatening, I returned into the palace, and after learning from the page on duty before Alma's door that she was sleeping, I lay down and in a moment was myself fast asleep.

And my rest was disturbed by wild dreams to which I had not the key, though psychology could to-day explain them. Always the same dreams haunted me in time of peril and difficulty. I had consulted some of the soothsayers and heard dif-

ferent interpretations which gave me no clue; these were actually my submerged memories asserting themselves over my
dormant brain.

Chandra, the hospital, Moreland and Mrs. Staines whirled
through them in a dervish dance. I saw them in their strange
garments and listened to their strange speeches; I saw New
York where Og's palace towered over the ruins, and through it
all I sought for Alma and never found her.

At last I started up, trembling and bathed in sweat, to hear
a confused shouting in the palace corridors. The sound was
taken up by the multitudes in the city. I grasped my sword and
ran out of the room. The corridors were empty.

I ran to the stairway that wound about the bronze Buddha.
The end of the passage, toward the hanging carpet, was packed
with a struggling mob of pages and servants.

In a moment they had broken and begun stampeding toward
me in wild flight, running down the stone stairway and filling
the courts below.

As they fled they disclosed Halkh and one of his archers
standing with bent bows before the door of the secret pas-
sageway. I ran toward them and saw that the passage, which
was illuminated by lamps, hung high on the walls, was filled
with armed men.

Mnerma rushed toward me screaming. She did not know
me and would have run past me, but I caught her by the arms.

"What is this?" I cried to her.

"My lord, forgive me!" she screamed. "It was for the princess
and him. He told me that if I would give him Kara's key to the
stone door he would bring me to rescue us. He lied; he tried to
hold me—"

"Go to the princess—" I began; but the terrified girl had
broken away and was among the pushing, scrambling mob on
the stairs. And I stood, sword in hand, before Halkh.

Six feet from us the captain of Timour's hosts had halted.

"Yield you now!" he began. "We war not on the Yuki, but on Og and his traitors—"

Halkh's great bow straightened, the arrow twanged and the captain fell, pierced through the throat.

With a rush the men-at-arms behind him came swarming up the stairs. And ever Halkh's bowstring twanged and that of the man beside him; and faster than our assailants could ascend the steps of the flight beneath us they fell, shot through armor and body, and helm and brain.

The shouting in the streets had increased in volume. In a brief interval Halkh turned to me.

"This was the meaning of the feints on the bridge, O lord," he said with a quiet smile.

And as four men sprang upward he discharged two arrows, and his companion two, and the four fell, writhing, down again, upon the bodies of their companions.

Suddenly a terrific clamor broke out almost beneath the palace windows. I heard the wooden timbers of the bridge reverberate beneath the rush of steel sandals. High above the sounds of the combat came the yells of the triumphant Yuki.

Then I heard a rustle at my side, and Alma stood with me, asking no questions, but laying her hand lightly upon my shoulder. As I turned my head momentarily I saw the hopelessness on her face. But through it shone her love for me, unquenchable and triumphant.

She darted from me toward the audience-hall. I knew that she had gone to summon the king. But it mattered nothing; it was only a question of moments. Down in the keep the archers were fighting desperately to hold off their assailants, ignorant, no doubt, of what was happening within the palace. How Halkh had learned I never knew.

For the arrow sheaths were empty. Halkh fitted his last shaft to his bow and fired. For a moment the Yuki halted, not understanding; then they came upward again, slowly and doubtfully; then they saw, and their movement changed to a rush that filled the tunnel from wall to wall and bore us back into the corridor.

Out from their ranks leaped Timour, in double steel, wielding his flashing yataghan. One sweep of it cut down Halkh's fellow-archer; yet before the blade fell Halkh had stooped and snatched the sword from the hand of the dead Yuki captain, who had been the first to fall.

I heard the mighty shout of Og in the audience-hall and plucked at Halkh's sleeve. He understood me and step by step we retired, while Timour, who did not seem to know me, and his men beat upon us from all sides.

Now we were behind the swinging carpet, in the room of the deaf and blind fife-players, who, standing motionless as statues, blew on their instruments with distended cheeks, ignorant of all except the ritual of their task.

Now we were at the entrance to the audience-hall. The hanging carpet swept across my face, blinding me for the moment, and Timour's blade tore mine from my hand. He raised his yataghan again.

Then Halkh, leaping between us, received the stroke, and toppled to Timour's feet.

Suddenly Timour knew me. He let his blade fall and shouted to his men, who sprang on me and bore me to the floor.

As I fell beside Halkh he opened his eyes and raised his hand weakly in salutation.

"The oath of Halkh—in life and death his lord's true henchman," he whispered. "For the Princess Alma's sake, whom I have ever loved, and who has never known it. Pardon, lord, and farewell!"

CHAPTER XXIII

THE VIAL

OVER ME TIMOUR'S Yuki swept into the audience-hall, and looking up I perceived Og on his throne alone. Not one of all those who had feasted with him had stayed during his last drunken slumber, when the end was at hand and even his two retainers had abandoned him, so that his arms, no longer upheld, had fallen over the sides of the golden chair.

Heavy with sleep, and bellowing like a herd of bulls, the old king saw the inrush of armed men and knew his destiny. It was the moment that must come to every Yuki king, he who gains his throne through the slaying of his predecessor, according to the old law, loses it in the same manner. I saw the great trapped giant stumble upon his feet and take his stand on the lowest step of his throne. His roars shook the great hall, he raised his unsheathed yataghan and as the Yuki rushed at him, he dealt death about him with every sweep of his weapon.

Blood and foam stained his face, blood of his foes covered him. He looked the incarnation of all that is at once heroic and abominable.

The Yuki were all about him, clambering upon the throne, striking from behind and either side, and the mighty sword clove them as if they had been clay.

"Come, Timour," he roared, "thou who wouldst be the king of Nork! Come hither and fight according to the Yuki laws, coward and traitor!"

Stung by the taunt, Timour sprang forward, but one of his

men flung himself before his master, with shield upraised, to receive Og's stroke. The great blade pierced through shield and armor, and the body beneath; and, raising the writhing form impaled on his yataghan, Og hurled it into Timour's face, flinging him to the ground. He raised his blade again; but before he could strike one of the Yuki standing upon the throne behind, plunged his yataghan through Og's body.

Og roared, and setting his huge hands to the steel plucked it out and hurled it from him. But a dozen swords were in him. Tottering, Og fell on one knee.

Even thus he surpassed Timour in height and all the men about him. He snatched a sword, rose, and went fighting backward toward the grille of the Buddha's jaws, and the swords that pierced his vitals stood out in front of him like a sheaf of corn. And fighting still he did not deign to utter a word.

The Yuki, gazing at him in terror and wonder, drew off and watched the great blade circling round his head. Smaller grew the circles drawn by the tired king; he stumbled, tottered and fell, his great head hard against the grille.

He spoke once in a whisper and it filled the hall with sound.

"This thing was written in the book of the wise man, Malachi," he said.

With a triumphant shout Timour ran forward and plucked Alma from where she crouched—behind the throne.

"Hail, princess of the ant people!" he cried. "I have found thee and to-morrow thou shall be Timour's handmaiden in his palace halls!"

He uttered a command, and I was raised from the floor and brought forward to where Timour now sat, king on the golden throne.

"Summon hither my counselors," he said, "for it is in my mind to dispose of a matter quickly."

The shouts rang through the palace. In came the Yuki and ranged themselves in their companies. There was no need to ask what had become of the keep's defenders.

Among them I recognized nearly all Og's leaders, now Timour's henchmen. And there were men who had marched out to battle with me, and old Epsilon and his priests, and Kara, alone and moving proudly as the prospective queen over the floor; and lastly the blind and deaf fife-players, who knew nothing of Timour's rule, as they had known nothing of Og's, but fifed as they had been trained in honor of their god.

Timour called Kara toward him, and his counselors arrayed themselves at his side. Then Alma and I were led forward by our guards.

"O men of Nork and of the Yuki," Timour began, "ye have seen by this change how fickle are the fortunes of princes. Verily, Og was a great king, and I his loyal servant; and yet, because he put shame upon me through the hands of this base-born clown, he forced me to deprive him of both life and throne. Nevertheless, he shall be buried with all the honors due to his rank, and we will enshrine him among our protective deities, that he may watch over Timour's fortunes from the land of the shades. This we will do, for Timour is a merciful prince."

From where I stood I saw the great head of Og against the grille. The open eyes that stared toward mine seemed yet to hold some flicker of consciousness, as if life had not entirely fled.

"Ho, Epsilon, come hither!" Timour continued.

The leering figure of Og's soothsayer came forward and made obeisance before the throne.

"What will my lord?" asked Epsilon.

"Epsilon," said Timour in mockery, "you are wise beyond all men in the lore of the sacred books, except old Malachi, the prophet of the ant people, who prophesies more truly than thou."

"Nay, O king," responded Epsilon self-confidently, "truly the magic of Malachi is as naught to my magic."

"Good!" grunted Timour. "Of that we shall take cognizance. You see the traitor, Ruuf, the swineherd's son, before me, and me on Og's throne. Think you that Malachi's, or any other magic can either deliver him from Timour's vengeance or unseat me?"

"Nay, O great king, there is no magic known that can deliver him from thine hand or unseat thee," responded Epsilon.

"Then it is in my mind, O Epsilon, to celebrate the old custom whereby a prince of the Yuki sacrifices a slave to the bronze Buddha whenever he takes a wife. And it is in my mind to take to me the Princess Alma, for I know well her stubbornness, and that in no other way than by fulfilling her law and becoming her husband can I obtain from her the vial whose drinking gives immortality and whose breaking brings about the downfall of the Yuki empire."

I heard a startled gasp from Kara. She stood still, staring at Timour, her face and throat dyed red with shame and humiliation. And all eyes in the room sought hers, for there was none present who did not know the bargain that she had made with Timour, and the reward for the treachery that was to have been hers.

But a greater wonder filled my mind than that at Timour's betrayal of Kara. She had not, then, given him the vial! She must have kept it in anticipation of just such a trick.

Twice Kara opened her lips to speak and failed, and the third time the words came falteringly.

"A boon, O king!" she cried, dropping upon one knee.

"Aye, ask, and it shall be granted thee, thou ever faithful one!" replied Timour ironically; and it occurred to me that Timour, for all his treachery, was wisely disinclined to take to him a wife of the like nature.

"Twice, O great king," began Kara, gathering vehemence as she spoke, "twice; O great king, has Kara been put to shame thus publicly among the Yuki. Now grant leave unto her to withdraw, that she may end her days peaceably in a far country, hiding the memories of her dishonor under the yellow robe of a nun."

"We grant thee this, O Kara," answered the king.

"Nay, but another boon! The king is great, and to be shamed by him is the chance of the king's favor. But to be shamed by a swineherd is more than Kara's meed. Grant, O king, that Kara may whisper to him some secret that she knows."

"What is this secret?" asked Timour indifferently.

"A woman's secret," answered Kara, "concerning his parentage, whereby his doubts may be stilled forever; for verily I have learned that he was never Og's son, but truly the swineherd's."

"We grant thee this, O Kara," returned Timour magnanimously, shrugging his shoulders as at a woman's folly.

Kara strode up to me with blazing eyes. She raised her right hand. I thought she meant to strike me. But, with a movement so quick that it passed unnoticed, her left hand found my own, and, while she pretended to whisper in my ear, I felt the vial slipped into it.

As my fingers closed upon it Kara turned to Timour once more.

"Kara's thanks unto her liege," she said. "And now, her mind being at rest, she will fulfill great Timour's boon and withdraw from his presence, happy in the knowledge that she has served her lord."

She swept down the hall and passed out beneath the hanging carpet.

"And now," said Timour to Epsilon, "know that it is my intention to delay no longer, but to be united in marriage to the Princess Alma forthwith. Therefore, let her maidens attire her in royal robes, and let the Buddha be put in readiness to receive his victim."

Epsilon, with a low bow and a smirk, departed to fulfill his portion of the command. He entered the passage that led to the jaws, and in a moment I heard the slow clank of the mechanism begin.

Alma, who had stood before Timour hitherto as one asleep, stepped straight in front of the throne.

"O my lord Timour," she began, "we, who are the sport of

war, must need accept its verdict. Yet since it hath pleased thee to grant these boons unto one who hath betrayed all, grant one unto me, who have betrayed none."

"We grant thee this, O queen," said Timour.

"Know, then," said Alma, "that never shall I be wife of thine, save on one condition only: and that is that thou spare the life of Ruuf, my lord, and suffer him to depart into his own country."

Timour glared at her, and the courtiers, astonished, began to whisper. Then Timour forced a smile upon his lips.

"Aye; but, O queen, if Timour grant thee this, where is the vial which I have coveted so long?" he asked.

Alma looked from me to Timour. And I cannot blame her if in the end her pledge seemed to her of less consequence than my life.

"It shall be thine, O Timour," she answered. "Now I have it not, but Ruuf, my lord, knows—"

"Call him not thy lord!" cried Timour angrily.

"—knows where it is. Yes, it was taken from him," continued Alma in agitation, "by treachery, but—"

"Fine words," growled Timour. "O queen, I give thee the life of Ruuf, the swineherd, for the vial. But let the vial be brought forthwith before the Buddha is ready for his sacrifice."

He signed to my guards and they hurried me along the passage toward the Buddha's jaws.

The metal gate had been drawn up, but the latticed grille was in place, and looking through it I could see the stone teeth already beginning to grind while the floor quivered.

Timour stood near me beside the body of Og. The giant lay with his head against the grille, as he had fallen, looking like a great trunk that has been blown down by the wind. Alma clung piteously to Timour's arm.

"Nay, but delay, my lord!" she panted. "It may be that the vial can be obtained speedily. Grant me that I may speak with Ruuf here—"

"O Timour, let thy heart's desire be granted!" I cried. "Truly the whereabouts of the vial are known to me, and if I be permitted to stand forward I can tell thee of it."

Timour nodded to the guards, who released me. I strode up to him, standing between him and Alma.

"This vial, which is said to confer immortality, O king," I began, "and also to portend, by breaking, the end of the Yuki realm, is in a place known to me." And, carried away by some impulse that made me reckless and seemed to raise me even above Timour and make me indifferent to him, I cried:

"Here is the vial, O Timour, and here thine empire endeth!"

And I swung the little bottle with all my force against the metal of the grille.

It cracked in my hands, revealing two little globules within, like quicksilver.

With a cry Alma, who had read my purpose, leaned toward me, seized one of them, and placed it to her lips, while I placed the other to mine.

And I flung the broken bottle at Timour's feet.

Timour stood motionless, looking at me. There was no wrath on his face, but a sort of understanding, as if something had come to pass against which he had armed himself in vain.

"Basil!" he cried.

And I knew him, and half-remembered and groped for memory and struggled to weave it into consciousness.

"Basil," he cried again, "is this the end? Give me the vial— give me another vial that I may drink of it. You did not know, Basil, if you had trusted me all would have been well. Now the end comes. Alma, the vial. I say! Another vial!"

The courtiers, astonished at their lord's outbreak, waited beside him. Old Epsilon, as if bereft of reason, rushed toward me. Somebody held him back; and all the while Timour raved.

Suddenly he saw Og's golden crown, which had fallen from the old giant's head, beside him, and recovering himself stooped to pick it up and place it on his own head.

And even as he stooped the giant form of Og uprose. The huge arms, outstretched, clasped Timour about the body. Og kneeled, he tottered to his feet, the swords still through his body; and whether in consciousness or nature's last automatic reproduction of an act I do not know, he began to swing Timour round his head as he had swung his yataghan.

He whirled him in the faces of the terrified priests and courtiers until he seemed to juggle a wheel; and then, with all his mighty force, he hurled him clean through the grille into the brazen Buddha's jaws.

The gnashing teeth caught him. He screamed, and above his screams came Og's last whispered words:

"This, too, was written in the book of the wise white man, Malachi!"

I felt out in the gathering gloom, found Alma, and drew her toward me. I pressed my lips to hers. I felt the hands of the infuriated priests upon me lighter than thistledown. And thus, holding each other fast, we went out into the darkness.

CHAPTER XXIV

SUBSTANCE AND SHADOW

THE GNASHING OF the teeth had ceased, but I could still hear the rattle of the chains. Then came a crash, as if the whole mechanism of the Buddha had smashed under some giant hammer. And in my ears there still rang Timour's last cry of agony.

I clutched at Alma, but my arm encountered emptiness. I reached out through the darkness, but she was with me no longer. I cried to her, but she did not answer me, and my voice fell light as a wraith's on my own ears.

Dimly, like shadows, I saw the raving priests and courtiers and the huge form of Og upon the floor, fading out of my vision.

Then, like a flat picture against the wall, there came into view the hall of Dr. Moreland's hospital.

I was standing beside the door of the automatic elevator, looking at something, and the night nurses were running down the stairs toward me, and others were about me.

"Mr. Clifford, don't look at him! There's nothing can be done!" cried the night porter. "I warned him not to use the elevator till it had been put into order."

"Him? Whom?" I asked, trying to remember what had been said and where I was. Names without meaning—Timour, Og, Epsilon—went racing through my mind.

"Mr. Raj!" answered the man. "He tried to get into the elevator, and it went up, and he slipped, and it crushed him against the sides. I heard you gentlemen talking loudly, and I was coming in to see if you wanted anything; then I saw you come out of the room a minute ago and go to the elevator. The accident has been a shock to you, Mr. Clifford."

One of the night nurses screamed; but it was not at the sight of Chandra's body, hidden under the night porter's overcoat. It was at Mrs. Staines standing on the stairs and peering over. How long she had been there, of course, I could not know; but she must have seen everything.

"Don't let her look!" cried the nurse in attendance on her. "There's been a little accident, Mrs. Staines—that's all. Mercy, won't you please go back to bed at once?"

"Oh, yes, I'll go back to bed," answered Mrs. Staines. "But I heard something happen, and I fancied somehow that there had been an accident. It's too late to do anything for him now, I suppose, Dr. Clifford?"

Then I shook myself together and the names that had been perplexing me vanished wholly out of my mind. I wondered whether I had been dreaming. And back into my consciousness crept all the events of the evening: our session, the *Cannabis saliva*, Mrs. Staines's irruption and—blankness.

I was astonished at the poise and self-possession of the woman, whose nervous malady had been closely allied to insanity.

"I'm afraid it is," I answered. "But won't you please let me take you back to your room, Mrs. Staines?"

"Oh, yes, I suppose so," she answered. And as Johnson, the senior surgeon, who lived close by and had been sent for, arrived just then, I went up to her. She took me by the arm as we went along the corridor.

"Dr. Clifford, did I say anything unfair to you this evening?" she asked.

"Why—not exactly, Mrs. Staines," I answered.

"I had a bad attack of nerves, and I remember going down to your room to expostulate with you about something, though I don't remember what it was, and I'm afraid I was very rude to you. The truth is, I took a dislike to you, Dr. Clifford. I don't mind telling you now, for it was just the sick fancy of a nervous woman, and I'm feeling better than I've felt since I've been in the hospital. I had an absurd idea—but perhaps I'd better not tell you."

"Don't be afraid of hurting my feelings," I answered, as we stood together at the door of her room.

"Well, I had an idea—I knew it was a delusion, but I couldn't shake it off—that we had once been engaged and you had jilted me. But I'm going into the country for a long rest soon, as I was telling poor Mr. Pal—he thought it would do me a world of good, too. What a terrible thing to happen, Dr. Clifford!"

I nodded, for I had liked Chandra, and the thought of his death had almost unnerved me.

"Well, we can't tell," she went on. "Sometimes people get their deserts when they don't seem to."

Her remark seemed to me so heartless that I made haste to leave her. When I got down-stairs Chandra's body had already been removed to the mortuary, and Johnson, in the house-surgeon's room, was puffing at his pipe nervously.

He questioned me a little about the accident and then we dropped the subject by mutual consent. I think Chandra had been too vividly in our lives for us to trust each other to speak much about him.

"By the way, Clifford," continued Johnson, "I want to try to get a final answer out of you about that partnership offer of mine. I've got the site for my hospital fixed and as good as purchased. It's over in Long Island, in the hilly part near the north shore. A splendid place, Clifford," he went on enthusiastically, "situated on a level plateau overlooking a valley, and excellent drinking water from a stream close by. We'll get all the *malades imaginaires* from Brooklyn, for I've got something of a pull over there, owing to my connections. What do you say?"

"No, thanks," I answered, greatly to my own surprise, for on the day before I had finally made up my mind to accept the offer.

"Why, what's the matter, Clifford? It's the healthiest part of the island. They say nobody's died there for years, and I'm going to advertise that in my booklet. You aren't going to throw away such an opportunity? And I assure you I need a man of your experience and temperament. I know what I want, and you're it."

"No, Johnson, I've thought it over and I've decided to remain on here," I answered.

"Well, I'm sorry, of course," he answered, a little stiffly, and soon after he bade me good-by.

Early next morning Moreland came bustling in, greatly upset by the accident and full of cross-questionings.

"You say you both went out into the hall together and that Chandra slipped and fell?" he asked. "I don't feel you could have helped that—in fact, something has come to my knowledge that makes me sure you couldn't; but I do blame you for letting him use that confounded elevator. I tell you the things are a constant peril to life. I'm going to have it taken out right away."

He fretted and fumed a little. Then I asked him:

"I suppose you wouldn't mind telling me what you meant about something coming to your knowledge?"

He took from his pocket the little bottle of *Cannabis*.

"Poor Chandra had given himself a hypodermic of this stuff," he said.

His words shocked me, for I had had a guilty feeling that if we had not both taken the injection the accident would not have happened. I had felt sure that I had been a little under the effects of it, for I had a dim remembrance of a rather vivid quarrel between us.

"Yes," said Moreland. "Chandra had been practicing on himself. I found the puncture mark in his arm. And this bottle was taken out of this room some time in the night by Mrs. Staines. The nurse found it in her room. You must be more careful, Clifford. I don't mean about that, but about doing what poor Chandra did. You're always practicing on yourself with drugs in just the same way. Does it make you happy to make these sacrifices?"

And as he spoke everything was made clear. My other life rushed back into my memory, yet with no stunning shock, but rather as the mellow remembrance that an old man has of his youth. And with it came the intense longing for Alma, which I knew could never be satisfied.

"Well, do take care of yourself," said Moreland as there came a tap at the door. "I can't afford to have you take those risks, because you are my most valuable assistant. I think a good deal of you, Clifford—I believe that must be my daughter. I brought her in with me this morning to do some shopping."

He went to the door with his long stride and opened it. Outside, in Paris gown and a big hat and long white gloves, the most bewildering vision that ever crossed my eyes—Alma!

"Dr. Clifford, my dear," I heard Moreland saying.

I bowed, and as we looked at each other I saw a faint red rise to the girl's cheeks.

"I'm pleased to meet you, Dr. Clifford," she said.

And that was all. But I knew—I knew that, as Malachi had said, in the end all would be well.

I knew that, having found her, I should never lose her again. And though I believe that, if what Chandra told me is true, neither of us may ever consciously know that life in Nork again, I would go through it a hundred times, if that were needed, to retain her. Yet even in this life I trust that some of those whom I knew there will come to me, linked by that friendship that rises into our hearts from the unconscious memories of other lives. And I shall search all my friends to see if one of them may perchance be Halkh, who died unrewarded, that I may know him and clasp his hand.

"And I hope—we hope," said Moreland, "that you'll come down to Northtree soon."

"I shall try hard to, Dr. Moreland," I answered.

ABOUT THE AUTHOR

I WAS BORN of an ultra-respectable English family inhabiting a solid middle-class district of London, and seemed destined from birth to pass through a public school and university, go to the Bar, and end my days as a high legal luminary.

There had never been any erratic character in our family, with the exception of an ancestor who served as interpreter to Napoleon, and is reputed to have spoken every language in Europe. I don't know whether it was some atavistic prompting that induced me to cut short my scholastic career and go to South Africa. But in any case, that was what I did.

I spent several years there, wandering through the length and breadth of the sub-continent, from Cape Town to the Zambezi, finally getting into the newspaper game in Johannesburg. It was through this newspaper work that I discovered I had the writing instinct.

This seemed to indicate America as my logical goal, and I made my way to New York, trying my hand at newspaper work, then joining the staff of a magazine, and finally beginning to sell to the magazines.

My first efforts were directed toward the highbrow magazines, but, even when successful, I was always working in a difficult medium. I could never understand why action was considered low, and, with Shakespeare and almost every other accepted writer on my side in this argument, I was delighted when I found myself able to crash *All-Story* and *Argosy*, through the kindly interest of the godfather of so many writers in this country, that revered and almost legendary character, Bob Davis.

This success enabled me to leave New York, and I spent the next four years among the *habitants* of Canada, seeing a good deal of the country, and writing mostly of it. Some fifteen of my serials in the Munsey magazines were subsequently published in book form in England. I have published a few highbrow novels for the fun of it (average sales, 300 copies), but I get more fun out of writing the straight adventure story than from anything else.

Victor Rousseau

Am at present living in Toronto, but regard this more as a jumping-off place than anything else, and am looking forward to extensive new travels as soon as circumstances permit.

THE ARGOSY LIBRARY ™

SERIES 1 INCLUDES:

* DENT * KETCHUM * KLINE *
* MacISAAC * ROSCOE *
* ROUSSEAU *
* SELTZER *
* TUTTLE *
* WIRT *
WORTS

THE BEST FICTION
FROM THE FRANK
A. MUNSEY LINE

GENIUS JONES
BY THE CO-CREATOR OF DOC SAVAGE
LESTER DENT

WHEN TIGERS ARE HUNTING
THE COMPLETE ADVENTURES OF CORDIE,
SOLDIER OF FORTUNE, VOLUME 1
W. WIRT

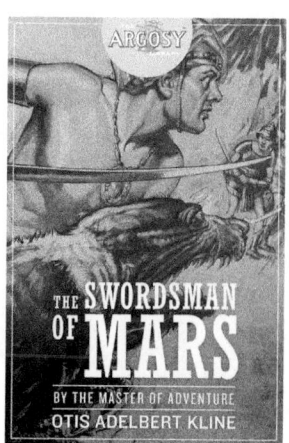

THE SWORDSMAN OF MARS
BY THE MASTER OF ADVENTURE
OTIS ADELBERT KLINE

THE SHERLOCK OF SAGELAND
THE COMPLETE TALES OF
SHERIFF HENRY, VOLUME 1
W.C. TUTTLE

GONE NORTH
BY ARGOSY READERS' FAVORITE
CHARLES ALDEN SELTZER

THE MASKED MASTER MIND
BY THE AUTHOR OF PETER THE BRAZEN
GEORGE F. WORTS

BALATA
BY THE AUTHOR OF THE RAMBLER
FRED MacISAAC

BRET-WALDA
BY ARGOSY READERS' FAVORITE
PHILIP KETCHUM

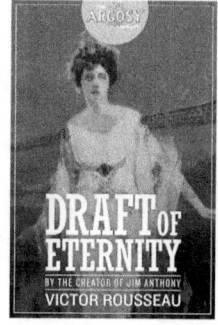

DRAFT OF ETERNITY
BY THE CREATOR OF JIM ANTHONY
VICTOR ROUSSEAU

FOUR CORNERS
VOLUME 1 • BY ARGOSY LEGEND
THEODORE ROSCOE

SERIES 1 • AVAILABLE SPRING 2015

www.ingramcontent.com/pod-product-compliance
Lightning Source LLC
Chambersburg PA
CBHW051835020726
47502CB00005B/1803